To remember
jaunts to Whidbey.
Enjoy
Sue

Final Impulse

Mystery on Whidbey Island

DAN PEDERSEN

FINAL IMPULSE

Final Impulse

Mystery on Whidbey Island
With Detective Shane Lindstrom

DAN PEDERSEN

Mysteries by the Author

Available from Whidbey Island bookstores and Amazon.com

Final Deception: *A Whidbey Island Mystery (Book 1)*
Final Passage: *Mystery on the Alaska Ferry (Book 2)*
Final Escape: *Mystery in the Idaho Sawtooths (Book 3)*
Final Justice: *Mystery on Whidbey Island (Book 4)*
Final Pursuit: *Mystery in the Adirondacks (Book 5)*
Final Impulse: *Mystery on Whidbey Island*

Other Titles by the Author:

Wild Whidbey: *The Nature of Island Life*
Whidbey Island's Special Places (not sold by Amazon)
Louis and Fanny: *15 Years on the Alaska Frontier*
Outdoorsy Male: *Short Stories and Essays*

R1 – Nov. 15, 2019
Cover image: *MV Kennewick* approaches Keystone Harbor, c 2019 Dan Pedersen
Email inquiries to Dan Pedersen: *dogwood@whidbey.com*
Copyright © 2019 Dan Pedersen
All rights reserved.

ISBN-13: 978-1695767904

Characters

Listed roughly in the order introduced

Shane Lindstrom – sheriff's detective, Whidbey Island
Elizabeth Lindstrom – Shane's wife, runs Eagles Inn B&B
Katarina (Kat) Brown – criminal justice student, Boise State University
Captain Gail Walker – ferry captain on Port Townsend crossing
Cordell Wurm – sex offender, Clinton, Washington
Nadya Komanesch – George King's Russian girlfriend
George King – Nadya's boyfriend, an engineer, lives in Greenbank
Grace King – George King's wife, works for software company
Dr. Ralph Emerson – County coroner
Zeke Kapinski – logger, Zeke's Wildcat Logging, Greenbank
Kweku and Adwoma Standish – Caretakers of a private Bahamas island
Tiff – nickname of Capt. Walker's friend from abused women's group
Annie – Capt. Walker's nickname from abused women's group
Donovan – An Island County deputy sheriff
Dr. Joyce Haycourt – George's audiologist
Dr. Bruce Haycourt – Joyce's estranged husband, urologist
David – Grace King's boyfriend, from Coupeville
Pastor Tom – Pastor of Prosperity Bible Church
Charity – Pastor Tom's wife
Charlie DeGroot – Board President, Prosperity Bible Church
Brad Haraldsen – Shane's friend, journalist, Stanley, Idaho
Irene Haraldsen – Brad's wife, artist and horse rancher
Robert Yuka – Governor's bodyguard, Boise, Idaho
Marie Martin – Robert's wife. Federal wildlife officer

Foreword

Final Impulse is book six in my Northwest mystery series, this time with Whidbey Island detective, Shane Lindstrom, as the central character. Kat Brown, a favorite of many who read *Final Pursuit*, is back to help Shane unravel the mystery.

This book stands on its own, but to read more about Detective Shane Lindstrom, please see the earlier books in this series. He is a central character in all five.

The story and all of its characters are entirely fictional. Some of the inspiration came from actual events on Whidbey Island, mixed with a large helping of fiction. The irony is that actual events sometimes are even more surprising than the wildest flights of fantasy. So rest assured, dear reader, that if you can imagine something, someone has already done it.

I owe thanks to all who provided assistance, especially two good friends who were the first to read the entire manuscript – Claire Creighton and Elizabeth Hall. One of the ironies of writing a book is that the author reads every sentence about one hundred times. We know the book so well that we read right past obvious errors and correct them in our minds. That's where fresh eyes are so important!

FINAL IMPULSE

Without a Trace

It was late afternoon and snowing hard as the Dodge 4x4 truck pulled onto the shoulder of a wooded roadside outside Greenbank, Washington, on Whidbey Island. A solitary figure in a black trail jacket got out and closed the door. The driver shivered in the cold air after the cozy warmth of the heated cab.

The driver stood a moment and listened for the sounds of other vehicles. Then, hunched against the snow falling on bare skin around the collar, the figure walked to the back, opened the tailgate and reached under the aluminum canopy.

The driver's hands found the cotton cord tied around a rolled-up rug, and pulled. The rug slid easily and thumped to the ground.

The driver was hoping no one else would come along on this secondary road for the next few minutes. It seemed unlikely there'd be any witnesses in this weather, in the gathering gloom of a winter afternoon.

Snow was falling so fast that the truck's tire tracks were the only ones visible. The blowing snow already had obscured part of the license plate, and the driver's own breath formed small puffs of white with the exertion of sliding the rug across a small clearing toward the edge of the trees. The driver's heart was pounding. The rug found a resting place in a low spot behind a bush.

Then, quickly, the driver returned to the truck and drove off. Already, snow was starting to cover the traces.

Into the Void

Shane Lindstrom stood in the forward lounge of the state ferry *MV Kennewick*, hypnotized by big snowflakes rushing at the glass. In this furious snowstorm, it was hard to say where sky ended and sea began. Visibility was maybe a hundred feet. The water was flat and gray, leaving them all but blind as the boat felt its way across the shipping channel of Admiralty Inlet.

It had started snowing an hour earlier, around 1 p.m., and most shops and offices in Port Townsend were closing early for Christmas Eve. The Island County detective wrapped up his business at the Jefferson County Courthouse and lost no time hurrying back to the ferry terminal to catch the next sailing to Whidbey Island. Daylight would be gone by four o'clock. People were eager to get home for the holidays and settled before the worst weather hit.

Shane had walked aboard the ferry that morning. He had a habit of leaving his car behind on the Whidbey side and going as a foot passenger. He didn't need his car for this trip, and by leaving it behind he wouldn't have to worry about missing his return trip if there were more cars in line than space on the boat.

He had gone to Port Townsend to meet with his counterpart in the neighboring county about Cordell Wurm, his chief suspect in five murders in the two counties over the past two years. The last had been three months ago – a woman Wurm had tried to date in high school. "I think he was taunting us with this one," he told the Jefferson County undersheriff. "Not only was she someone he knew, but her body was found a mile from his house. If you can catch him on a security camera near the scene of one of your victims, or link him to her, it could break this case open."

The victims all were women, their nude bodies dumped by

rural roadsides. Shane believed the killer was going back and forth on the ferry, committing his crimes in two different police jurisdictions. What really clinched it was that one of the Jefferson County bodies had been found on Whidbey Island. Whether this was to confuse the police, or for the killer's convenience, Shane just couldn't say.

Wurm had a history of domestic violence, sexual offenses and other crimes, but Shane wasn't ruling out other suspects. His department was keeping an eye on 23 registered sex offenders in Island County, and scores of others who had histories of arrest and complaints for domestic violence.

Wurm, from Clinton on Whidbey Island, had an alibi but a flimsy one – that he had spent the nights of the murders smoking marijuana with a friend in his mom's garage. She was an alcoholic, and he worked off-and-on as a roofer. Wurm had a long history of fighting. He was wiry and strong, quick to take offense, and seemed to enjoy bullying, beating people and inflicting pain.

He had dropped out of South Whidbey High School a few years earlier after getting his younger sister pregnant. By then he had also served some jail time for selling drugs. It struck Shane that most classes have at least one bully and a small group of anti-social losers who hang out together to smoke and drink, and cause trouble.

Wurm was the leader of this group in his class. Over the years, Shane had watched Wurm grow more hardened as a small-time criminal and drug user. He enjoyed beating people so badly they had permanent injuries. Some of his teachers confessed fear of crossing him and were relieved when he moved on.

He was surprisingly cunning, and his modus operandi seemed to be evolving. Shane could tell he was learning from experience. He was good at covering his tracks, paying cash for most purchases. Shane had reviewed records of all calls placed to, and from, Wurm's cell phone around the time of the murders and it appeared Wurm was turning off his phone for long periods so it couldn't be traced.

Of all the acquaintances Shane had interviewed, none could remember Wurm having a normal, healthy relationship with a female. In fact, they said, he seemed to carry a lot of anger toward women in general.

That anger, and Wurm's inability to account for his whereabouts at the time of the murders, and his lack of a healthy relationship with any woman, including his own mother and sister, kept Shane coming back to him as a suspect in the serial killings.

It depressed Shane to think of how many men – the predators were almost always men – hid their dark secrets and psychological dysfunction while going about daily life alongside the rest of society. Wurm could be a chameleon when it served his purposes. When the opportunity presented itself for damaged men to take something they wanted, they crossed the line.

Out of habit, Shane sized up his fellow passengers as he watched them come aboard the ferry. The boat was carrying maybe a dozen cars, one motor home and a logging truck, a fraction of its 64-car capacity. Just two other passengers shared the lounge with him, one of whom was quite short, practically a gnome, with a ratty, two-foot-long beard, wearing a checkered shirt and dirty overalls, held up by suspenders. It was hard not to notice him.

Shane was pretty sure the guy with the scruffy beard was the truck driver. He imagined how easy it would be for a driver who goes back and forth on the ferry to commit murders in two counties. With the self-loading rigs, many of these loggers worked alone. It would be easy to bring some extra baggage back to Whidbey after working on the peninsula.

The guy was pacing and his eyes darted around nervously. Shane wondered if he was looking into the face of the killer right now. Shane had noticed a red stain on the truck's running board. It could be anything, such as blood from hitting a deer or the result of a skinned knee. Just out of thoroughness, he had noted the name on the truck, Zeke's Wildcat Logging, Greenbank, WA.

The other passenger in the lounge was a nicely dressed, young woman in wool slacks, white blouse and a tan raincoat, sipping a cup of vending machine coffee. Shane imagined she was a Port Townsend shopkeeper returning to her home on Whidbey. Like Shane, she was a walk-on.

Zeke, if that was the logger's name, seemed to be stealing glances at her a little more than normal.

Shane wondered if they were conscious of his interest – if he looked like a lawman to them. He was tall, with a full head of black hair and a neatly trimmed beard, in khaki slacks and a white shirt with a tie. Wisely, he had worn a blue, goose-down jacket today instead of his navy blue sport coat.

The bulk of the down jacket concealed his badge, which was

clipped to his belt, and the bulge of his shoulder holster and sidearm. As he was going out the door that morning his wife, Elizabeth, had made him laugh. "You still look like a cop – one who's trying to pass for a regular guy."

Maybe it was the confidence – the way he carried himself, on duty or off.

Right now Shane wanted to put it all behind him for a few days and enjoy the holiday.

He couldn't remember another Christmas Eve as magical as this one was shaping up to be. The hard part of any cop's life was to turn off the job for a little while and relax with the family, but the ferry ride in the snow was putting him into the mood to be home by the fireplace.

It was would be nearly dark by the time Shane reached his car on the Whidbey side, brushed off the snow and started the twenty-mile drive south to his home in Freeland. He knew road conditions were worsening by the minute and it would be icy. The forecast called for a heavy snowstorm – a foot or more – followed by winds and an Arctic cold wave. It was a recipe for widespread power outages.

All he wanted now was to get home to his wife, Elizabeth, for a week of turkey, dressing and apple pie. The Eagles Inn B&B was both their business and their home, but for Christmas week they'd have it all to themselves, and a special guest. If they lost power, there was always the cozy warmth of the woodstove, and the backup power of their generator.

He pulled his cell phone from its holster on his belt, saw only one bar, and dialed Elizabeth. She answered on the second ring, but the static was bad. "Hi honey," he said. "I'm on the ferry. We're not going very fast, but should be in Keystone Harbor soon. Look for me in about an hour."

Elizabeth said something Shane didn't catch in the garbled transmission. "I'm sorry, what?" he asked. He listened, still wasn't sure, but took a guess and replied, "Yes, it's beautiful out here in the snow – really magical and cozy. But eerie at the same time. There's hardly anyone on the boat. I suspect they may shut it down when it gets back to Port Townsend because visibility is so bad."

He added, "When we get to Keystone I'll have to brush and scrape my car. I won't be setting any speed records down the highway, but I'll see you shortly. I love you."

When she didn't reply, he realized the call had been dropped. He hung up, wondering how much of that she had heard.

*

On the ferry's bridge, one deck above Shane, Captain Gail Walker stared at her radar and GPS. She knew the ferry's exact position and the location of all the tankers, containerships, fishing boats and military vessels entering or leaving Admiralty Inlet. The instruments on these new ferries were the best she'd ever used. But this was the most treacherous crossing in the state's entire system, often shut down for wind, fog, currents or tides.

A former lieutenant commander in the US Coast Guard, Walker wore her brunette hair close-cropped. At five-foot-eight she carried herself with the same erect military bearing she'd perfected in the service. Being responsible for a crew primarily of men, she took a no-nonsense approach to her duties and projected the image of a focused professional. It gained her their respect.

The Coupeville – Port Townsend crossing was known to be the most difficult in the state's system, and only the best captains were assigned to it. Walker was proud to be one of them.

What worried her tonight was the remote possibility of a hapless powerboat or small sailing vessel at mid-channel in this whiteout, with no GPS and no radar receptor. It wasn't likely, but to assume otherwise was the kind of sloppy thinking that got captains in trouble. The last thing she wanted for Christmas was to capsize another vessel and take someone's life.

The captain had posted a lookout on the bow and another with binoculars beside her on the bridge, but they would be little help in visibility like this. She blew the ship's whistle every thirty seconds and listened carefully for a response, but none came. It seemed they were the only vessel out here this afternoon. The mate was on the radio to Puget Sound Vessel Traffic Center. This was simply all they could do – this and run slowly.

As the ferry neared Whidbey, Walker picked up a solid echo from the blasts of the ship's whistle. It confirmed what her radar already showed, that they were coming up on the steep bluffs of Admiralty Head. She reduced speed but maintained enough to have good steering control. That was the tricky thing about Keystone

Harbor. You wanted to slow more in preparation for landing, but didn't dare. Currents around the harbor entrance were so tricky that even the most skilled captains sometimes ran aground on the sandy bottom.

She was right where she needed to be. Captain Walker's GPS guided her straight into the tiny harbor's pinhole entrance. Ahead, in the fading light, she could make out the dark shapes of the wing walls, loading ramp and cross arm with its red, flashing lights.

A solitary figure in a yellow slicker and orange safety vest stood by the ramp and pushed the control to raise it a few feet, since the boat was riding higher than last trip on the incoming tide. A handful of cars waited in the holding area for the return trip to Port Townsend. The boat was behind schedule but would make up some time with a quick turnaround here.

Shane stood on the bow and watched the two deckhands loop mooring lines around cleats on the boat. Then he hurried up the ramp to his car, a white mound in the snow by the roadside. He was glad he had driven the Subaru Outback today because it was as reliable in snow as any vehicle he'd ever owned. He used his arm to brush snow from the windshield and rear window, then started the car and let it warm up and melt additional snow on the window glass.

Snow on the road was about four inches deep, and in most places the tire tracks of other vehicles had packed it down. He put the car in gear and pulled onto the road. The Outback seemed right at home on this surface.

When Shane reached the main north-south highway he turned right, toward Freeland, doing thirty miles per hour. Drivers apparently had taken the road warnings seriously because traffic was light to non-existent. Halfway to Greenbank he met an oncoming Dodge truck with an aluminum canopy. That was about all till he got to Freeland, with its bright lights, gas stations and shopping plaza.

Moments later he was coming up the drive to the Eagles Inn. The lights of home cheered him, but he was even happier to see the cozy fire in the woodstove and the glass of wine Elizabeth handed him. "Sit down for a minute but don't get too comfortable," she said. "You need to meet the airport shuttle in thirty minutes."

*

As the shuttle rolled to a stop at the Freeland Shell gas station, Shane stationed himself by the door. Several groggy passengers got up from their seats and started forward in the aisle. They were the first to get off. Then, Shane saw Kat Brown appear from the back of the van and descend the steps, wearing a big smile. Shane caught her and wrapped his arms around her.

"Welcome to Whidbey Island," he said.

"And to a white Christmas," Kat added.

"That, too."

They walked around to the back of the shuttle, where the driver was unloading suitcases. Kat claimed her backpack and small suitcase, and they trudged through the snow to the Subaru, where Shane piled Kat's luggage into the back of the car. Then they headed for the inn, as snow continued to fall.

"Kat, I'm so happy to see you!" Shane exclaimed. "It's been a couple of years. How have you been?"

"Really good," Kat replied. "I love Boise State University, though I miss Brad and Irene, and Bolivar. I see them every chance I get, but studying keeps me pretty busy."

Kat's cell phone dinged and she pulled it out to check her messages. Shane glanced across and saw her smile.

"Just a second. I have to answer this," Kat said. "Somebody wants to know if I arrived safely."

Shane's ears perked up at the word, "somebody."

Pock pock. Pock pock pock pock, she typed rapidly with two thumbs. In a moment she finished and put the phone away.

"Have you chosen a major yet?" Shane asked.

"I have," she said, smiling again.

"Let's have it."

"Brace yourself. Criminal justice, with a minor in sociology."

"Seriously?" Shane replied.

"Seriously."

"I love it!" he declared. "Have you told anyone else? Man, do we ever have things to talk about."

"I thought we might."

Shane was thrilled, even if the news came as a complete surprise. That Kat would become a cop like him had never crossed his mind, but it was the perfect choice for her. She was bright and resourceful, with all kinds of street smarts – handling situations that might intimidate others.

At six-foot-two, and slender as a gazelle, Kat was still as Shane remembered her from their original meeting in the Adirondack Mountains of New York. But the smile was new and Shane liked it. She had grown her dark brown hair to her shoulders and he liked that, too – it softened her.

She'd been a homeless teen when Shane's friend, Marie Martin, tackled her outside Elizabeth's vacation getaway place in the Adirondacks. Kat had fled her abusive and alcoholic mother and had been living by her wits, breaking into unoccupied cabins at Pursuit Lake for food and shelter. But Shane and his friends found her bright and likable. Notwithstanding everything, she had a moral code he respected. She was a person of integrity and basic honesty. It was Elizabeth's idea to take a chance on her, inviting her out to Idaho to start a new life on the ranch of their friends Brad and Irene Haraldsen, in Stanley. She was well on her way now, Shane thought.

As they pulled up in front of the inn, Elizabeth came down the steps with her arms open wide to welcome Kat and exchange hugs.

"It's so good to be back," Kat said. "I had forgotten how beautiful it is here since my brief visit when you first brought me out here. Is Billy around?" she asked, referring to Shane's fourteen-year-old son.

"He's spending Christmas with his mom," Elizabeth said. "He has really grown up in the last few years. We'll stop by and see him while you're here. But this Christmas, you'll have to help us make some memories. Now, let's go in and get out of this cold, and find you a spot by the fire for a glass of wine."

First Date

At the darkened Greenbank General Store, the airport shuttle stopped again. The driver's manifest indicated only one passenger was getting off here. He set the brake, got out and watched as a thirty-something blonde came up the aisle and descended the steps. She was wearing heels and a red miniskirt beneath her fur jacket – quite pretty, he thought, but over the top. She was European, perhaps. Certainly no islander home for the holidays.

As he retrieved her suitcase from the luggage compartment he noticed she was looking around, anxiously. Nearby, a black Lexus LS 570 idled, parking lights on, and an older man in a bulky jacket stood next to it – her father, perhaps.

"Nadya?" the man called to her.

"Meester King?" she replied, walking toward him.

"Please, just George."

He gave her a hug, holding for an extra beat, and rubbing her back.

"Merry Christmas," he said.

"Merry Christmas, George."

People were so interesting, the shuttle driver thought. Everyone has a story. He wondered what little drama this encounter was about, but he had a schedule to keep and the weather was closing in.

He climbed back into the van, closed the door and pulled onto the highway again, with one last glance at the couple in the rearview mirror. Once he got to Oak Harbor with his five remaining passengers, his shift would be over and he could go home for the holidays.

*

"The snow is stopping," Shane called through the open door from the inn's front porch. "The sky is full of stars and the wind is picking up. Now the night gets interesting."

"Close the door, will you?" Elizabeth replied. "That wind is cold."

Elizabeth and Kat relaxed by the wood stove in easy chairs. After a big meal of roast turkey, cranberry sauce and dressing, everyone was letting down.

Shane rejoined them, settling into a chair of his own. "If the forecast is right, it'll get into the twenties tonight, with winds gusting to fifty or sixty. I really don't expect to have power in the morning, so keep an extra quilt handy, Kat."

"Well, we have lanterns and flashlights, and a nice stove," Elizabeth said. "And you have the week off, so bring it on."

*

Nadya sat demurely in the passenger seat as George drove. The headlights illuminated the white, snowy ribbon of highway and some of the roadside. Her first impression was positive. He was maybe ten years older than her and distinguished, with gray hair, and was as tall as she was. He had dressed in a white shirt and tie to meet her, which seemed a good sign.

In his letters and phone calls he gave the impression of a nice man. His voice over the phone was soothing. She knew he was well established as a civil engineer. But meeting someone like this, on the other side of the world, was a huge leap of faith. He had paid for her flight here and described Whidbey Island as heaven on earth, but tonight, in the dark, after a long and tiring trip, she just thought it seemed isolated.

Still, it couldn't be as isolated psychologically as where she'd just come from. Chelyabinsk, her industrial hometown, was one of the Big Eight large-diameter pipe producers in Russia, not where Nadya wanted to grow old and die, either as a low level employee or the wife of one. Her father, grandfather and grandmother all worked in the plant and lived together in one overcrowded apartment. Her mother had died three years ago of cancer likely linked to industrial chemicals to which she'd been exposed. It had been wrenching to watch.

Granny was stooped and defeated, Nadya thought, by the loss of her daughter and a lifetime of hard work and sacrifice that led only to more of the same. Nadya was numb about her mother's death. She could see herself becoming her grandmother unless she did something to break the cycle.

Not that the pipe factory was the only opportunity for a pretty young woman who wanted more from life. The city also produced electrodes, tractors and machine parts. Nadya wanted none of that. She wanted more than a factory or secretarial job till she died.

Ironically, what had really put Chelyabinsk on the map was the Chelyabinsk "Event" of 2013. It was a superbolide meteor the size of a six-story building that exploded in the atmosphere about sixteen miles above the city. Meteor fragments rained down and caused damage over a vast geographic area. More than a thousand people were injured. Such disasters never seemed to happen in the United States.

As George drove, they passed a few houses that looked warm and inviting, with Christmas trees in the window. The farther they drove, the fewer the houses.

"Did you have a good flight?" George asked, rousing Nadya from her deep thoughts.

"Da. I mean yes," she replied with a little giggle.

"Give me time. I'll learn the language," George replied. The conversation went quiet again. He reached out his right hand and took hold of hers, and they entwined fingers like two lovers just starting to explore each other.

"I'm sure you are nervous," George said after a moment. "I am, too. This is something new for both of us. But we're good people; it'll be okay."

Nadya looked at him and smiled softly. The reality of what she had done in coming here was sinking in. Did he have expectations or an agenda that she wouldn't recognize until it was too late?

George turned up a narrow lane in the trees. Nadya saw no more houses and wondered how much farther it might be.

Her gut said she could trust this man, but she was always thinking ahead. If this went terribly wrong, where could she run?

There were no neighbors. Even if she did find a house, what would she say? "I am from Russia and I make fool. Help me!" Would they even open the door for her? In Russia, everyone minded their own business. People in rural areas like this were often simple and odd. She couldn't quite picture a sophisticated man like George living in such a remote place instead of the city. Had he lured her into a trap?

"Sometimes you just need to take a risk," George said. "Give love a chance. You're single. I'm separated. We both want someone with whom to share our lives."

Nadya had come a long way since posting her profile on the international dating site. If this worked out, it could be the start of a much better life in the United States.

George pulled into a clearing and stopped the Lexus in front of what looked like a government official's dacha.

"This your house?" Nadya asked. It seemed like a palace to her – huge and all peeled-log construction, with a green metal roof, like pictures she'd seen of the best homes in Alaska. There were lights at every window, a three-car garage, a large lawn and manicured landscaping, with lights to illuminate the shrubs and trees. Only in America do they have lights for trees, she thought.

"Come in and I'll show you around. Let me just get your suitcase from the back."

George reached for the suitcase and led Nadya up the single concrete step to the front door. She noted that, like a gentleman, he opened the door for her and let her go through it first.

The house was breathtaking – spacious and uplifting, with a vaulted ceiling in the living room, and stained-glass windows. She couldn't believe George lived here by himself, after her childhood in the drab and crowded apartments that are normal in Russia. She marveled at the hardwood floors, Oriental rugs and textiles hanging from the walls.

But something about the house struck her as odd.

It was the woman's touches – all the art, candlesticks, figurines, framed pictures, vases and embroidered dishtowels. If the outside of the house had looked masculine, the inside was decidedly feminine.

"Your wife," she began, "you are getting divorce?"

"Yes, we're in the process," George said. "It takes a while."

"She's gone how long?"

"Oh for some time. I don't hear from her at all."

"You need to, what is the word, redecorate more manly," she said with a little laugh.

Nadya could still recite some of George's profile from memory. *Unattached male, professional, engineer, virile and youthful, seeks adventurous partner, thirtyish, for walks on the beach, cozy dinners, romantic getaways. Thinking marriage.*

It all sounded good and she liked the word "marriage," but everything hinged on that other word, "unattached."

Nadya continued her tour of the house.

"This door," she said. "Is for where?"

"The garage and workshop," George said. "I keep it locked.

"Let me show you the bedroom," George said, leading her in the opposite direction and down the hall.

Nadya noted the king bed looked like it had been made up by a man, not too precisely. That was typical. Working as a maid in a hotel, Nadya had learned to make perfect hospital corners. She had also cleaned up after many guests who had behaved like animals and left their disgusting fluids on the sheets. That was the seamier side of her job.

She wondered what it would be like to make love to this man tonight in this bed, in this room. They hadn't discussed the sleeping arrangement in their letters and calls, but the long-distance flirting and sexual tension were high. Of course, it's easy over the phone for the mind to fill in some details that don't always conform to the real world.

Her girlfriend, Vanya, said she was a hopeless romantic. It was probably true. Nadya wanted a storybook love – maybe a little too much. She had always believed it was possible to have it if one worked hard enough and was willing to take risks. She was a softie at heart.

Maybe George would be a gentleman and put her in a guest room for the night, but she couldn't imagine that would satisfy either of them. They had come too far. Best to get the sex out of the way fast. It would answer some questions, and then they could both relax.

She hoped he would like it. She knew how to please a man. Love was so hard to find – a good, well-balanced relationship. But this was America, the land where all things were possible, and she was one step closer to her dream.

*

In the woods a hundred feet from the house, a man lowered his binoculars and let them dangle from the strap around his neck. His long white beard nearly covered them and kept his face warm against the cold, but his Stihl baseball cap didn't provide much protection for his bald head.

He blew warm air into his hands and rubbed them together against the cold. He had watched the couple arrive, and watched through the windows as the man led the woman from room to room. When she took off her fur coat, her red miniskirt sent a rush of warmth through him. Watching people is addictive, he thought, and you never knew what surprise might be just around the corner.

He had been watching the house for weeks, studying routines and learning about the man and woman who lived there. This was not that woman. Something exciting was happening here. He just didn't know what it was.

Earlier, he had watched the man's truck back into the garage. Someone loaded what looked like a heavy, rolled-up rug into it, and then the truck drove away in the snowstorm.

He could get into trouble if he got caught watching; he knew that. Maybe if he had a normal relationship with a woman he wouldn't do this. But without that relationship, watching people was the next best thing.

The Cruel Season

Dr. Joyce Haycourt stared at the empty bed that had seen the whole history of her marriage, like a missile taking off and then falling back to earth. Her husband, Bruce, a urologist, had filed for divorce in November, citing irreconcilable differences. Winter was the cruelest season. Days were short and nights were long. She had never felt so alone. With no children and no family in the area, Christmas just made the misery worse.

The problem between them wasn't one thing but everything. They were consumed with their separate careers, and their personal habits drove each other crazy. Joyce knew that her earwax removal routine pushed all of his buttons. She left the apparatus on the kitchen table, probably a passive-aggressive gesture on her part. The table was the one island of tidiness in the house she knew he considered sacred space.

For her, the flashpoint was the bathroom sink. The trimmings from his beard in that sink infuriated her. He was obsessive about his precious beard – a narcissist about his personal grooming.

Eighteen years had made them hard and bitter toward each other, but Joyce was reluctant to give up on their marriage. She suggested counseling. Bruce said it would do no good. He no longer loved her and, in fact, had fallen for one of the younger surgical nurses at the hospital, who could talk for hours about the male reproductive system.

He bought a Harley-Davison motorcycle and started reclaiming his youth, riding all over Coupeville in black leathers with his young babe hanging onto his back. Joyce often saw the motorcycle parked in front of Toby's Tavern.

Bruce had told Joyce that vasectomies were his cash cow, but she knew what really inspired him was the challenge of digging out tumors and repairing inguinal hernias. Bruce hadn't vacationed with her in seven years. He had moved out December 1 to share a small cottage in Coupeville with his nurse.

Joyce wanted nothing so much as to prove to Bruce she was still desirable and attractive to men. She had gone back to everything she ever knew about flirting in high school.

She immediately started dating and thought she had found the ideal replacement for Bruce right away. In fact they'd had intercourse in this very bed on their first date, something she'd never thought possible in her wildest dreams. She felt liberated by it and had started planning her future with him. Her plan was to get married before Bruce did. But the man she had found was still married and had stopped returning her calls.

*

Three blocks from Joyce's home, it was the best of all possible times at Prosperity Bible Church. With extra services and a seasonal upsurge in the congregation's sense of generosity and obligation, Christmas was peak season for offerings, and the charismatic pastor anticipated a windfall over the next few days. The church's rock band had prepared a special Christmas concert of up-tempo holiday tunes sure to put the congregation into a happy mood.

Whidbey Island, with its large Navy base, was the perfect setting for his church and his brand of preaching. But he had learned from experience to always have a backup. He was operating in a gray area, ethically and legally. Things could go wrong fast.

The pastor had just one thorny personal issue that demanded urgent attention. Other than that, Christmas was his favorite season and he expected to do very well.

*

Three thousand miles to the southeast, Kweku Standish gave thanks for his good fortune. He and his wife, Adwoma, celebrated Christmas Eve alone, listening to holiday music over the short wave radio. They were the only fulltime residents of their tiny island in the Atlantic, with the complete run of a luxury home powered by large propane generators. The owner, a rich American, had never visited but it was their job to maintain the house in good working order toward the day when he might show up with little notice.

It wasn't a very hard job, given that they'd never even met the boss.

Kweku, a string bean of a man, was the handyman, groundskeeper and chief of security. Though he had no special training, he was especially proud of this latter responsibility and wore a mail-order badge in case someone set foot on the island and needed evidence of his authority.

Adwoma was the cook, housekeeper and maid. She called Kweku "Slim." He was a practical joker who looked at the sunny side of life and was perpetually upbeat by disposition. Adwoma, plump and jolly, took special joy in her cooking, and pampered her husband with his favorite meals. She harvested coconuts and pineapple right off their own trees.

"We've got to put some fat on dem' ole bones of yours," she liked to say. For that, she served him mashed potatoes and gravy.

"Ah, woman, you wan' me look like you."

"And what's wrong with dat?"

The island was quiet now, but a few months ago it had been noisy and dusty. They had hosted five men with chainsaws and a bulldozer, who had carved a six thousand foot gravel runway across almost the island's full width. Kweku sensed something was about to change.

The men had brought the bulldozer ashore in an old, World War II landing craft, lowering the ramp on the sandy beach by the island's marina. A barge carrying propane visited the island every few months to refill their big storage tanks. Most of the time, the propane crew and the monthly mail boat were the only visitors they saw.

Home Alone

Captain Walker guided the MV *Kennewick* into the slip in Port Townsend at 6:48 pm and watched from the bridge as a handful of trucks and cars from Whidbey Island drove ashore with the usual *bang bang* of front and rear wheels crossing the steel loading ramp. It had been a sloppy crossing with clouds of spray and white water breaking over the bow and washing onto the car deck. With such a light load, the deck hands had parked the cars back from the bow so they wouldn't get splashed with sea spray.

She had kept the bow into the wind as much as she could, but had to run broadside to it for several minutes at one point. The boat rolled steeply from side to side. Over the public address system she asked passengers to remain seated, and apologized for the ride. She was glad there were only a few tonight.

With the weather worsening, the ferry system already had decided to shut down the run for the rest of the evening after the boat got back to its main base in Port Townsend. With no further crossings remaining on her shift, Captain Walker was released early to go home, exactly where she did not want to be. The boat was where she felt confident and in control.

A single woman, she had expected to spend Christmas Eve on the boat with her crew. She said goodnight to her first mate and the deck hands, most of whom lived in other towns and would sleep on the boat tonight. She wished them a happy Christmas.

Then she put on her overcoat, walked up the ramp from the car deck, and started up the hill to her little bungalow on Lawrence Street, overlooking the waterfront. She loved this old town with its Victorian homes, brick buildings and sea-faring heritage. It was especially pretty in the snow, with Christmas lights decorating some of the houses and yards. It was filled with historic vessels. John Steinbeck's old sardine-seiner, the *Western Flyer,* was being restored here right now by boatrights skilled in wooden boat construction. She met only one other pedestrian on the windy, twenty-minute walk, one of whom was out with his dog. She paid attention to dogs more than their owners, and recognized this one.

"Merry Christmas," she said to the man.

"You, too," he replied. "Feels like a wild one."

Walker resumed her walk, looking over her shoulder from time to time, studying the shadows and the empty sidewalk. It was a habit she had developed several years ago. She kept her hands in the deep pockets of her overcoat. The fingers of one hand were wrapped around a can of Mace. From one of the houses she passed, she could smell the aroma of Christmas Eve turkey.

Like other crew members, sometimes Walker took her car to Whidbey when there was a shift change and she had somewhere special to go, such as Seattle. Several captains lived on the island. But she hadn't taken her car tonight.

Walker reached her darkened porch, fumbled for the key and opened the door with a scrunch. She had not left the light on, expecting to be on the boat this evening. Coming home to a dark house always made her nervous. Even though she had a restraining order against her old boyfriend, she always expected one day he'd be waiting for her.

As she stepped through the door, a blood-curdling yowl startled her.

Walker flipped the light switch. It was her big tabby cat, Tom, letting her know he was mad about her absence.

"Just hold on there, Thomas. I'll get to you in a moment."

Walker went from room to room, turning on lights and checking closets. She had no Christmas tree or decorations, but a well-lit house made her feel better. She opened some canned food for Tom and put it on the floor by his water dish. He went right to work on it. Then she poured herself a glass of wine.

Christmas is an especially hard time when you're alone with no plans and no family. Her parents were both deceased. She felt the need to talk with someone tonight and thought she'd call her friend, Tiff. That wasn't her real name but it was her nickname from their support group, and part of the code they used to conceal their identities if the wrong person saw a note or a cell phone contact and grew curious.

Walker had chosen "Annie" for herself, a takeoff on Tugboat Annie, though most people probably assumed it was from Little Orphan Annie. "Tiff" and "Annie" had met in a community group for women who were victims of domestic violence.

Everyone had secrets, she thought. Walker had never told anyone in the ferry system about the boyfriend who had abused and stalked her. She never would, because a captain could not be seen as weak or vulnerable. She and Tiff did not know each other's real names, nor where each other lived or worked. For their own protection, those topics were off limits in the group.

She dialed the number but Tiff's phone went right to voice mail and Captain Walker left a message: "Hi, this is Annie. Just thought I might catch you. I got off work early tonight and am sitting here bored to tears. Call me if you feel like a talk. It doesn't matter how late."

Walker was surprised Tiff hadn't picked up. She was stuck in an abusive marriage and would probably be as lonely as Walker on a night like this when all the emphasis was on family and joy. Maybe they'd catch each other later.

Like Walker, Tiff was a professional. One would never expect her to get mired in an abusive relationship. But trouble has a way of sneaking up in little steps, and by the time one realizes how bad it has become, finances and emotions are so entwined it can be almost impossible to unravel them.

Walker had met her ex-boyfriend in the Coast Guard and wasted eight of her best years trying to make the relationship work with him. They'd been to a relationship counselor but nothing had changed. He was her senior officer and she knew it was a bad idea to start a relationship with him, but disregarded her caution and did it anyway.

They had bought this house and lived together for a time. She liked that he was handsome and decisive, an officer on the way up. What she hadn't realized at first was how controlling and violent he could be. He was stationed now in Port Angeles, much too nearby, and living there in an apartment. Getting him out of her life had proven more difficult than anything she'd ever tried to do.

Walker sat down in her recliner and leaned back. Tom jumped

onto her lap and arranged himself in a compact circle, with just his long, front legs protruding, to push and play with her hands. It was their little game. He flexed his paws against her gently. He was already vibrating – purring – and it was making her drowsy.

"Merry Christmas to us, Tom," she said.

Outside, the wind whipped at the treetops and a streetlight threw shifting shadows across the closed curtains of her house.

Lights Out

The lights went out at 2:43 a.m. Shane had been lying awake, listening to the wind and the crunch of trees crashing together as they swayed. Elizabeth, a sound sleeper, was getting a full, restful night. Shane, not so much. He leaned over and kissed her on the forehead. She did not open her eyes, but, by the light of the moon, he thought he saw a little smile.

The house was still. He slipped out of bed, opened the drawer of his bedside table and felt for the headlamp he kept there. He found his pants and shirt, and put them on. With the light on his head, he made his way to the living room and opened the woodstove with a clank. The coals of their Christmas Eve fire still glowed bright and orange. Shane added three chunks of dry fir to the firebox and closed the door. He loved the smell of wood. A lick of flame appeared and danced by the wood he had added. In half-an-hour, the stove would be good and hot. Elizabeth could cook breakfast on it.

He grabbed a warm parka, stuck his feet into his boots, and reached for his high-powered, police tactical flashlight. Then he stepped out into the biting wind and started down the road. He swept the light back-and-forth along the power lines, looking for trees and wires that were down. He knew from experience that sometimes a downed wire on his own property could leave the inn dark, even while the neighbors enjoyed normal power. If there was a problem nearby, he wanted to find it and report it to the power company.

Near the turnoff to his driveway he came to a tree lying across the entire road, but it had not taken down any wires. The outage was somewhere else. If it was the main transmission line at Deception Pass, the whole island could be dark.

He'd come back at daybreak with his chainsaw. Till then, no one would get in or out – not that anyone wanted to do either on Christmas Day.

*

The morning dawned bright with all the new snow to reflect the sun. Shane loved the view across the rolling terrain, through the trees and down to the sheltered waters of Holmes Harbor. It was especially magical in the snow, in the soft, rosy light right after the sun came up behind him.

Snow not only softened the view but also absorbed much of the sound, adding to the sense of peace. He put on sunglasses, fueled his saw and headed down the road, his boots squeaking as he walked. It took him only a few minutes to de-limb the tree and buck it into firewood-length rounds. He rolled the rounds to the roadside and made a neat stack, thinking he'd probably leave them there till spring. Such was life on the island, where people were a little more self-reliant.

On the way back, his work done, Shane stopped to listen to a Great-horned Owl in what he called his "owl tree." He found it about thirty feet up the large Hemlock, on a stub of branch near the trunk, its ear tufts fiercely pointed, and its yellow eyes looking right through him.

This was mating season for the largest of the island's owls and he never tired of their early-morning conversation. Somewhere in the distance, a female answered with a distinctly different call. It must have been a rough night for those two, he thought.

Shane and Elizabeth were lucky to have twenty acres with the inn. They had left most of it natural as wildlife habitat – a tangle of trees and brush, nurse logs and old snags full of woodpecker holes, with lots of places for wild creatures to nest and forage for food. He often thought the Hippocratic Oath should apply to island residents, "First, do no harm." The natural instinct of many newcomers from urban places was to eradicate nature. Thankfully, after people had lived on the island for a while they began to appreciate nature as one of the benefits, not one of the drawbacks.

Shane and Elizabeth both loved studying the birds and wildlife. It was the best thing about living in a place like this that still had many acres of forest. Many of the deer, squirrels and birds on their land had learned to trust them, and approached the inn with little fear.

Two hours later, Shane was relaxing by the woodstove with Kat and Elizabeth. "This is the life," he said. "No work, no power, no lights, no TV and nowhere to go."

"And nothing to do, eh?" Elizabeth added with a wry smile.

It was just like olden times, Shane imagined, when his ancestors came west on the Oregon Trail with no electrical devices to complicate their lives.

He loved watching these two women. Kat and Elizabeth were reading by the soft glow of several oil lamps, with light blankets over their knees. Kat's book was *Postmortem*, Patricia Cornwell's debut novel about a medical examiner investigating the strangling of a woman in Richmond, Virginia. Shane watched Kat grimace every so often when she came to a gruesome detail. Elizabeth was reading *Crow Country*, by Mark Cocker. She was not grimacing but reading choice passages aloud to Shane and Kat.

It was Elizabeth who had come up with the idea to take a chance on Kat – bring her out West to live with their friends in Stanley, Idaho, and start a new life. Elizabeth had an uncanny sense about people and she sure got it right with Kat.

It was a leap of faith but it had transformed Kat. She had been living by her wits in the woods of the Adirondack Mountains at Pursuit Lake, where Elizabeth owned a century-old family retreat. Kat's big mistake, which was also probably the best thing that ever happened to her, was in breaking into Elizabeth's Adirondack house and getting caught by their friend, Marie Martin. Kat was a refugee from an alcoholic mother. Elizabeth took a liking to Kat and could see she had no future if she stayed there.

Watching Kat and Elizabeth this morning, they seemed so content. Shane didn't want to admit he was bored and wanted to get their noses out of their books.

He took a sip of coffee, put down his cup, and declared, "Kat is majoring in criminal justice – did you know that?" He looked right at Elizabeth.

She glanced up from her book, over the top rim of her reading glasses. It was her Meryl Streep look – the one that Shane loved.

"For real?" Elizabeth asked. "You want to be a cop?"

"I do," Kat replied. "I actually learned quite a bit about crime and housebreaking during my years of cabin prowling. I was doing ok till I broke into your house, which was full of cops!"

She grinned sheepishly.

"Rotten luck, eh?" Shane laughed.

Kat screwed up her face and stuck out her tongue an inch.

Shane made a face back at her. "Still, you landed on your feet."

"That's what Kats do, you know. What really threw me was that you and Shane and Robert and Marie weren't anything like I expected. You went out of your way to help me. I saw what it was like to do something positive in life and knew that's what I wanted for myself, too."

Robert was Shane and Elizabeth's friend, an Idaho State Trooper. He was an Alaskan Inuit and called his wife, Marie, his "white chick." She was a federal wildlife officer currently taking a break from her career to raise their young son, Martin. Marie had caught and tackled Kat when she tried to flee after returning a canoe she had either stolen or borrowed, depending on how one defines what she did. For Kat, that tackle was the first step in becoming part of this group of friends who had done so much to help her.

"It takes a strong heart to do what they do," Elizabeth offered, putting down her book and leaning forward. "They see the worst of human nature. Somehow, Shane manages to leave it behind most days and not bring it home."

Now that Kat and Elizabeth were talking, Shane was pleased with his little intervention. He sat back and listened.

"Does Shane's work take an emotional toll on you?" Kat asked.

"You might think so, but only if I have some reason to worry about him, and most of the time I don't. He's smart when it comes to taking risks, and such a good husband and father, I'm just thankful I found him. I'm intensely proud to be married to him."

Kat smiled. Shane liked how this was going.

Kat's cell phone dinged again. She glanced at it, smiled, and said, "I'll get that later."

"What about you?" Elizabeth asked. "You've been out west now for three years. Do you miss home and your mom?"

"I wish I could say I do, but this is my home now. I don't believe things would be any better between Mom and me if I went back to the Adirondacks to visit. I pinch myself every day now because I'm so lucky to have the life I do. If I went back to see Mom, she'd still be a prisoner of alcohol and those awful men she brought home. There was no future for me with her – and no future breaking into houses."

Elizabeth nodded.

"Maybe I'll go after I finish school. It'll probably just piss her off that I'm becoming a cop.

"Actually," Kat added, "I have an ulterior motive for spending Christmas with you. Of course I wanted to see you. But I was also hoping Shane would let me tag along on some of the cases he's handling," she said, looking his way. "Anything I can learn in the real world will help me with my studies."

Shane was at full attention now.

"I'd love that!" he said. "But you may see some things that aren't very pleasant. My main case right now is several murders we think are the work of a serial killer. Are you sure you are up for that?"

"Absolutely. If I'm going to be a cop, I'll need the stomach for it, and what better way to find out?"

It was the answer Shane fully expected from her.

"It won't be all work and no play. It'll give us a chance to look around the island, too. There's a lot to see here."

Remains

The body was lying in a low spot in the brush at the edge of the woods, a hundred feet back from the road. It was rolled up inside an Oriental rug, with one frozen arm jutting out to the side in rigor. Shane imagined that arm was protesting, "Stop!" Snow still covered most of it.

Power had come back on at the inn at 4:27 a.m. the morning after Christmas. Shane had awakened to the clicking and beeping of the answering machine resetting itself, and the brightness of unexpected lights in the house. He had gotten up to reset all the digital devices – the clocks, electric range, microwave and other appliances – and never gotten back to bed.

Now it looked like it might be some time before he slept again.

Elizabeth and Kat had made a big breakfast of bacon and eggs on the electric range. Shane had washed the dishes and then they had all settled into a day of leisure. It was early afternoon when Shane's cell phone rang, with only about two more hours of good daylight remaining. The three of them were playing Monopoly, and Elizabeth was cleaning up with New York and Tennessee avenues, and a slew of houses.

Shane got up and took the call. "Another?" he exclaimed, scribbling on a notepad. "I can get there in 15 minutes." He listened some more, said it was no problem, and hung up.

"Two women found a body in the woods by Greenbank," Shane said. "They need a detective. I'm really sorry we can't finish the game."

"I'll bet you are," Elizabeth said.

"Can I go along?" Kat asked.

"It might be pretty bad. I don't want a dead body to be the

memory you take home from Christmas."

"Please! I can handle it. I'm going to become a cop. Let me go."

"Ok," Shane said. "But just remember, you don't have to look at anything you don't want to see."

The day had dawned sunny with the deep blue sky typical of cold weather in winter, but the roads were icy after the snowfall. With the clear days and cold nights, the surface ice had partially melted and then refrozen, slicker than ever. They took the Outback but even it did some sliding. Shane turned on the rotating red and blue beacon on his dashboard. When they reached the scene, on a secondary road outside Greenbank, two sheriff's cars and the coroner's van were parked by the roadside. A deputy was stationed by the road to direct traffic around the scene; he waved them to the shoulder.

Near the edge of the trees, Shane could see several deputies in the olive drab fatigues of Island County sheriff's officers, two women in civilian clothes, and a dog that looked like a Border Collie. His office had already set up a tent and lights, with a generator to power them.

Several crows watched from perches in the nearby trees, waiting patiently, Shane assumed, for everyone to leave. He thought it ironic that birders called a flock of crows a "murder."

Shane and Kat got out and crossed the clearing to where the group was standing. It was the arm that got his attention. It was frozen in position but the skin was starting to soften in the morning sun. If it hadn't been protruding so much, the rug might have gone undiscovered longer.

"Who found the body?" he asked.

"These two women here," one of the deputies answered. "They were out walking, which is their normal routine."

Shane introduced himself to the women and explained that Kat was an intern studying criminal justice, who was shadowing him. That was a little thin for allowing a civilian at the crime scene, but it seemed to satisfy everyone.

"How did you find the body, so far off the road?" he asked.

"Max found it," one of the women replied. "My dog. He has an incredible nose. I thought maybe he had found the carcass of a deer or some other disgusting thing, and called to him, but he wouldn't come. So we trekked across the clearing to this spot and saw the arm sticking out of the snow. We knew right away this was no deer under the snow. I was curious and brushed away some of it. Then I dialed 911."

The women said they walk the road almost every day as part of their exercise routine. There usually isn't much traffic and they enjoy the fresh, forest air. They're often so busy talking they don't study the ground very much, but Max does that.

Shane thanked the women and turned to Kat. "What do you make of it?"

"Looks like the body has been here since at least Christmas Eve, judging by the snow that was covering it. There was a little snow underneath the rug, so it was left here after the storm started, and a lot more on top of it, so most of the storm happened after it was left here.

"Rigor had already set in when the killer dumped it, because that arm was sticking out at an angle. If he'd been able to tuck it inside the rug, I think he would have."

"Good," he said.

"Any thoughts about the killer?"

"I think he was rushed because this is not very professional. The body wasn't hidden very well. It was probably disposed of in a hurry."

Shane was running through scenarios. Could this be the work of his chief suspect in the serial killings, Cordell Wurm? He also wondered about the logger he had seen on the ferry, Christmas Eve. Lots of trucks went back and forth regularly on the boat, so if a trucker were behind these killings, there were plenty of candidates. If this was a Jefferson County woman, the logger could have driven straight here from the boat and dumped the body. The timing would have been just right. It played games with Shane's mind to think that he could have been on the same boat as the killer and the body.

The coroner was standing by for instructions.

"Can you unroll that so we can have a better look?" Shane asked.

"If you don't want to see this, Kat, just step away." She did the opposite and leaned forward.

The rug was stiff but the sun had softened the fabric enough for the coroner to unroll it and reveal the body, which was still frozen.

The coroner folded back the rug as far as the thaw would permit. Shane could see the woman was about thirty-something, with dark, closely-cropped hair. She was nude and her face and skull were badly bashed. She looked fit. He suspected the killer had deliberately smashed the face to make identification difficult. She had no rings, bracelets, tattoos, scars or other distinctive marks. He could see no bullet wounds, though it was impossible in these conditions to be sure.

He turned to the deputy in charge of the scene. "Have you found a cell phone, or any eyeglasses, cigarette butts, papers or other personal effects?"

"Nothing at all," the deputy said, "but we're still dealing with several inches of snow. We'll search again when the snow melts."

"Check the missing persons reports for any leads on who this might be. And go over the rug for fibers, too – anything that might give us a clue about where it has been."

He hesitated a moment, then added, "Find out what you can about Zeke's Wildcat Logging, here in Greenbank. Don't mention the murder investigation – just get me some background on Zeke and his possible whereabouts."

"New suspect?" the senior deputy asked.

"No, it's just a crazy hunch, based on very little. He was on my ferry, Christmas Eve."

Shane thought a moment, and then added, "Find out about Bob's Boatworks, too." He was remembering a pickup truck with a canopy that had rolled aboard his ferry. He assumed Bob was a Whidbey resident who made his living building or refitting boats in Port Townsend. It would be easy enough to do that and maintain a residence on Whidbey, especially if one had a place to sleep on weeknights. On weekends, Bob could commute back across to Whidbey on the ferry.

Shane turned to the coroner. "Give me a complete report as soon as you can on cause of death. I need to know if there was sexual assault. That was the case with the other victims. And check for drugs and needle tracks. Let me know if she was a smoker or vaper. When did she last eat, and what was it? See what you can tell from the fingernails and condition of the hands. Can you give me a window for time of death?"

"Almost impossible," the coroner replied. "In these

subfreezing temperatures, normal formulas for cooling mean nothing. But I think your friend here has a good fix on when the body was left here. I can tell you there's been very little decomposition."

"Do what you can – give me a range. I appreciate it."

For Kat's sake, Shane was thankful the body had remained frozen.

Looking at the senior deputy on the scene, he asked, "Find out what our friend Cordell Wurm was doing over Christmas, and where he has been." The deputy nodded.

He turned to Kat. "I think we're done here for now. We can go back home and resume our Christmas holiday for a little bit, before the next shoe drops."

They made their way back to the car, got in and closed the doors. Shane pushed the button to start the engine and get the heater running again.

Shane sat a moment, then asked, "Was that pretty upsetting to you, seeing the body in that condition? That was more than just a body; it was an especially gruesome one."

"The reality hits you hard," she replied. "Not like on TV. I won't lie and say it didn't bother me. But at the same time, when I decided to major in criminal justice, I knew it would be my job someday to examine crime scenes like this. I'm glad I went with you on this one. I found out I'm pretty strong."

Kat let the warm air wash over her. The breath from their lungs was fogging up the windows. She watched the defroster clear two small circles on the windshield, and the circles gradually grow larger in diameter.

"That was fascinating," she said. "I'm sorry about what happened to that woman, but it's a real puzzle to piece together."

"That's what I like about this work – solving the puzzles and stopping it from happening again. We know we've had a serial killer active on the island for several months, but don't know if this case is part of that. There are some key differences here that we have to take into account."

"Such as?"

"None of the previous victims were bludgeoned, with their faces damaged, and none were rolled up in rugs. Maybe the rug was just for convenience this time, but the bludgeoning raises new questions."

Kat agreed. "I think it's possible the killer knew the victim and was trying to make it harder for us to establish a link that would lead us back to him."

"So is this murder related to the serial case?" Shane asked. "Or is this a crime of passion and rage?"

"The latter, I think. Whomever the victim was, she did not deserve what happened," Kat said. "We owe her as much justice as we can provide, given that we cannot give back her life. A few days ago she was living her life, doing all the ordinary things we take for granted."

"And then very abruptly someone took that away," Shane said. "So who did it, and why?"

Post Mortem

Coroner, Dr. Ralph Emerson, opened a refrigerated compartment and pulled out a tray containing the corpse of the deceased. He checked the toe tag for identification, then lifted the body onto a stainless steel exam table.

No matter how many times he did this he could not get over feeling he was violating the victim's privacy in the most intimate way. He reminded himself the body was just the empty shell of what had once been a human – that the spirit was gone from this body and it was not a person anymore, just skin and bones. There was no one remaining to feel embarrassed or violated.

In a murder case he liked to start with the hands, but in this instance it was impossible to ignore the jutting arm. He could only assume the arm had lain in that position for a time before rigor mortis stiffened it, so it could not be tucked inside the rug. She did not appear to have offered any meaningful resistance to the attack.

The hands reinforced that thinking. Hands typically reveal a great deal. He found no defensive scrapes or abrasions on the hands or arms of this woman. Often he would find bits of the attacker's skin and DNA under the fingernails, but in this case there was none.

Her hands were soft and free of calluses, suggesting she was a homemaker or worked in a professional capacity, but did not do physical labor with her hands like a carpenter or landscaper. Her skin showed no sun damage, which would be another sign of outdoor work. She was fit and trim.

He then moved to her head, where all the obvious damage to the body had occurred. He counted at least ten high-impact wounds to the brain and face. They were deep and round. From the angle of attack he believed she must have been lying on her back when the blows struck, most likely asleep, in that she made no effort to defend herself.

He measured the depth. The attacker's weapon had penetrated about two inches into the head. Death probably had been almost instantaneous with the first blow to the brain. Damage to the face had been secondary, perhaps to make it more difficult to identify the victim.

He carefully inspected the rest of the body. There were no needle tracks or other wounds. There was no indication of recent sexual activity or assault. The woman had no tattoos or piercings other than in her ear lobes for earrings.

The internal examination showed no contents in the stomach, consistent with the doctor's thinking that she had been asleep and had fully digested her last meal. Internal organs showed no signs of drug or alcohol use. The lungs were clear; she was not a smoker. He did find the beginnings of arthritis, especially in her right elbow, not unusual for a woman in her thirties, suggesting she played tennis or used that arm heavily to operate a computer mouse.

*

"It was sobering," Kat said when she and Shane reported back to Elizabeth on the body in the woods. "Nothing really prepares you to examine the body of a healthy person who was going about her life just a few days before. But Shane is pursuing several good leads and we're working on possible profiles of the killer."

Shane smiled at the word, "we," but had to admit Kat had pretty good instincts and ability to analyze a situation. He agreed with everything she'd said at the crime scene.

"What's next?" Elizabeth asked.

"We're waiting for a call from the coroner with the autopsy report," Kat said. "That will tell us a lot more – rule some things in and out. Personally, I think the victim is local and the body wasn't moved far before the killer disposed of it."

"So," Shane said to Elizabeth, "we're back in Christmas mode for a little bit."

"Why do I think it won't be long till I lose both of you?" she replied.

Just then Shane's cell phone rang.

"Lindstrom," he answered, and then listened for a moment. "Uh huh. Did you check Port Townsend, Anacortes and Skagit County? Well shoot. It was worth a try. Uh huh. Well, thank you for getting back to me so fast."

"That was the office," he said to Kat. "We don't have any reports of a missing female in the victim's age range. She may be a visitor from the mainland who ran into foul play. Or from Jefferson County. Or maybe she's a local who's been missing such a short time that no one has thought to report it yet. Let's see what the coroner says."

*

While they waited for the coroner's call, Shane suggested they call Brad and Irene Haraldsen in Idaho. Their mutual friends, Robert Yuka and Marie Martin, and their young son, Martin, were spending the holidays at the Haraldsen ranch in Stanley.

Shane had met Brad, a journalist, when he came to Whidbey Island a few years earlier to investigate the death of his college classmate, Bella Morelli. Brad and his artist wife, Irene, owned a horse ranch overlooking the Stanley Basin, one of the prettiest places on earth.

As Brad and Shane worked together on the case, a friendship developed that had grown in the half-dozen years since. A year after investigating Bella's death, Brad and Irene found themselves by chance on the same Alaska Ferry as Shane, and helped apprehend the suspects in Bella's murder. Robert Yuka and Marie Martin had joined them in that effort. Since then Brad had developed lymphoma and was currently undergoing immune therapy treatment in Boise.

Shane dialed the number and listened as the phone rang loudly on the other end. On the third ring, Brad picked up in his typical, strong, baritone.

"Brad Haraldsen."

Shane listened to that voice and imagined the body behind it. He knew Brad had lost a lot of weight in treatment.

"Brad, it's your old partner in crime, Shane Lindstrom."

"Hearing your voice is music for the ears," Brad said. "Do you have Kat with you?"

"As a matter of fact I do, and she's my new crime-fighting

sidekick. We're working on a heckuva case, and you Stanley people are missing out."

"I was afraid of that. We leave you alone for one vacation and you find someone new to take our place."

"Here. I'm going to switch to speaker phone and put Kat on the phone so she can tell you all about it," Shane said.

"I'll do the same at this end," Brad replied.

Kat explained it was a murder investigation, possibly a serial killer case, spanning two counties connected by a ferry crossing. She also mentioned she had decided to major in criminal justice at Boise State University, which brought cheers and congratulations from the group gathered around the phone in Stanley.

"So I'm having my dream vacation," she said, "tagging along with Shane. What about you?"

"Oh, we're having a rip snorter of a time," Robert replied. "We're playing Monopoly on the dining room table and Marie is cleaning up."

"That's what we were doing, too," Kat declared, "only it was Elizabeth."

Robert and Marie were a fascinating couple, Shane thought. Robert was an Inuit native and former Alaska State Trooper, currently with the Idaho State Police and assigned as the governor's driver and bodyguard. He was short, stocky and solid.

Marie had been a federal wildlife officer when they met Brad and Shane. Marie was trim and slim, a runner, and good with a firearm. She was currently on break from her work to raise their young son during the preschool years.

Fate brings people together in unlikely and unexpected ways, Shane thought. This group of friends had rescued Kat from a life of homelessness and petty housebreaking, and set her on a path to a good life and a fulfilling career. In many ways they had become the parents and family she never had.

*

It was 4 p.m. when the doctor called Shane. "Are you ready to take notes?" the coroner asked.

"Ready."

"The deceased is a healthy woman age thirty to forty, judging by development of the bones and teeth. She had arthritis deposits consistent with an adult of that age. She was going to need carpal tunnel surgery before too long."

"How do you account for that?"

"Too much tennis. Or it could be from heavy use of a computer."

"Go on."

"Death was caused by trauma to the head with a blunt object. The first blow probably killed her, but she was struck at least six or eight more times. Her face was attacked last, after she was already dead."

"What kind of blunt object?"

"The fractures of the skull are round. It could have been the head of a household hammer, or a crowbar with a hook, garden tool or some other implement that doesn't come to mind right now. Something heavy, swung with force."

"Lots of bleeding?"

"Oh absolutely, yes. It would have been an unholy mess of blood and brain tissue splattering all over."

"Sexual assault?"

"No. She hadn't had sex recently, and there were no injuries to that area. There was no evidence that this was a sexual attack."

"Had she ever had children?"

"I would say no."

"Did she defend herself – fight back?"

"No. Nothing under her fingernails. There are no scratches or other marks on her body that could have been inflicted by fighting or struggling. I don't think she knew what hit her."

"Was she attacked from the front or back?"

"Overhead, I would say. Not from behind."

"So possibly in her sleep?"

"That's what I'm thinking."

"Had she eaten?"

"Her stomach was empty. That would be consistent with a morning attack on someone who'd been sleeping all night and had lots of time to digest."

"Toxicology?"

"A trace of alcohol, maybe a glass of wine. No drugs. No needle tracks or other indications of prior drug use. No prescription pills that showed up in her blood."

"Time of death?"

"I think about two or three days ago. The body had started to decompose, probably from being indoors for a time before being moved to the freezing outdoors. Once it got outside, of course, all decomposition stopped."

"What can you tell overall from looking at her?"

"Well groomed. Took good care of her fingernails and toenails. I think she took pride in her appearance."

Shane let it all sink in for a moment.

"Okay, thanks, doc. This is helpful. I'll let you know if I need anything else." He pushed "end" on his cell phone and turned to Kat, and gave her the complete summary.

Then he asked Kat, "So what do you think? Random attack by a stranger, or domestic violence?"

"Well, apparently it wasn't a sexual assault," Kat said, "given that she hadn't had sex. I lean toward domestic violence by someone who had no interest in sex with her, and who didn't plan things very far ahead."

"It does look personal," Shane said. "I'll give you that. Ordinarily, I'd agree completely, but given the recent series of killings, I have to consider it's the work of a serial killer. I'd like to be able to pin it on Cordell Wurm but it doesn't entirely fit the profile of the other murders."

"So what are we missing?" Kat asked. "Could the killer be a woman? It feels like a disorganized crime of passion. Plus, it's Christmas, which is a terribly stressful time for many people. If someone's going to snap from the stress, this is the season."

She thought a moment, then added, "It could be a copy-cat killing to throw you off."

"That crossed my mind, too," Shane agreed, looking down at his hands. "It would not be hard for a woman to murder someone who was asleep. The victim was wrapped in a rug, which breaks the pattern. I still think it could be Wurm. I'm trying to keep my mind open and you raise good points."

"I'm thinking of another scenario, too," Kat added. "If the victim was from outside the home, and this is a serial case, we should be asking where he finds his victims. What do the victims have in common?"

She continued, "Abused women make good victims, so we

should consider evening classes, community groups and other places where victims gather to talk about their experiences and fears. Those are good places for predators to screen their victims."

"Where did you learn all this?" Shane asked.

"I read a lot. Don't forget, I grew up in an abusive home with an alcoholic mother and a whole series of her loser boyfriends."

"Well here's one thought to hold onto. If the killer was as rushed and disorganized as you say, odds are he made some mistakes at the crime scene. Or she did. We just need to find where it is."

Invisible Man

The deputy rapped hard on the door. A rug-rat dog erupted into a fit of barking over the din of the TV. The volume came down; a moment later, the door opened and the dog shot out.

"Oh for god's sake," Cordell Wurm moaned.

The dog locked its teeth around the deputy's pant leg and ripped a tear in it, but didn't find skin. The deputy shook it off with some kicking while Wurm stood by and watched.

"That's enough," Wurm said at last. Looking at the deputy, he asked, "What the hell do you want?"

"We like to remind you we're always thinking about you."

Wurm was wearing blue sweats and a rumpled, white T-shirt. The smell of beer was on his breath and in the room behind him. The deputy noted Wurm hadn't shaved for several days and his hair was greasy.

Wurm shifted his weight to one leg and rested his hip against the door frame, as if he didn't have the energy for this. With his wiry physique and long, stringy hair, he didn't have to try very hard to achieve the chip-on-the-shoulder look.

"I need to ask you a few questions," the deputy explained. "Could we talk inside?" he asked as he took one step forward.

"No, let's talk right here," Wurm said, blocking the deputy with his arm.

"We're investigating a crime and I need to know where you've been the last few days, and who can vouch for your whereabouts."

"The answer to your first question is the Olympic Peninsula, and the answer to your second question is 'no one.'"

"Can you be more specific?"

"I'd had my fill of people and Christmas music, so I got out of

Dodge for a couple of days and went for a drive. Christmas is my least-favorite holiday. So I packed up the pooch and did a loop of the peninsula."

"In all this snow?" the deputy asked.

"That's right. I'm a good driver."

"And that took how long?"

"Christmas Eve and Christmas Day. I got home late Christmas night. Had to take the Edmonds and Mukilteo ferries, because Port Townsend doesn't run late enough."

"And you saw no one?"

"Just some motel clerk in Port Angeles."

"Which motel?"

"I didn't notice. They're all alike. I paid cash and threw the receipt away."

"And you just drove all this time?"

"No, I did some hiking and beach walks. I remember Kalaloch was one of them, and Fort Worden."

"And you didn't meet anyone?"

"It's a pretty quiet time at the beach."

"Did you buy gas or eat in a restaurant?"

"The gas was all self-serve. The restaurants were drive-through, where you're just a voice on the intercom."

"So you can't think of anyone who might remember seeing you?"

"Not a soul," Wurm said. "I'm the invisible man."

*

"Wurm was being evasive. He has no alibi," the senior deputy said when he called Shane that evening. "Says he hates Christmas and took a road trip to get away."

"I think he likes jerking our chain," Shane remarked. "Where did he go?"

"According to him, he did a complete loop of the Olympic Peninsula in the snow, and stayed in some motel in Port Angeles whose name he doesn't remember. Paid cash. Threw the receipt away. He stopped several times, did some hiking and walked some of the ocean beaches – Kalaloch and the beach at Fort Worden in Port Townsend."

"That's fishy as hell. Nobody does that in the snow. Do we have a missing person's report yet from Island or Jefferson counties?"

"Nothing."

Wurm had been nothing but frustrating from the start. The latest victim, a former cheerleader, had graduated from Wurm's high school class. Her nude body was found three months ago by a roadside in Possession Point State Park, a mile from Wurm's residence. Another of the Whidbey Island victims was a teller at the bank where Wurm had an account. She told a friend Wurm had asked her out, but she said no because he was revolting.

Shane interviewed several former classmates who said Wurm seemed to have a crush on the cheerleader. But old crushes don't prove anything. Shane had questioned Wurm hard and couldn't catch him in a slip or shake his denials. He just sat there with his arrogant smugness and batted Shane's questions right back at him.

Wurm's link to the latest victim was the strongest of several coincidences that pointed to him as the killer. Shane had searched Wurm's house and property with no luck. Wurm seemed to take special delight in having vague alibis.

He was on the Olympic Peninsula around the time each of those victims disappeared, their bodies later to be found by roadsides on South Whidbey. But then lots of people went back-and-forth on the ferry. It was highly circumstantial, but maddening. Shane couldn't prove anything. He was pretty sure Wurm had murdered those women and would continue to kill until Shane stopped him. But in the back of his mind, Shane wondered if he had allowed Wurm to distract him from searching for the real killer.

He shifted his attention to other possible suspects.

"Have you had time to look into Zeke's Wildcat Logging?" he asked the senior deputy.

"Just a little. It's a sole proprietorship – no employees. Zeke Kapinski lives in Greenbank and does small logging jobs mostly on the Olympic Peninsula."

"Married?"

"No. Lives alone. But we turned up something quite interesting."

"Yeah?"

"He *was* married for two years when he lived in Forks. His wife disappeared in 2017. There was evidence of foul play – blood. The sheriff investigated but never found a body and couldn't link Kapinski to her disappearance. He claimed he was away on a small logging job the day she went missing. Her family insists she was afraid of him and that he murdered her."

Shane sat up straight. "Interesting."

"The property was a challenge, forensically. Kapinski kept chickens and did his own butchering, so there was blood all over the yard and on the axes he used. There were chicken feathers floating around, since de-feathering is part of the job of butchering. Here's something odd – he had a dozen chicken heads hanging from a clothesline. He also kept several pigs and they rooted and dug holes all over the place."

"What about the wife? Was any trace ever found?"

"There was blood in the house that indicated she'd been murdered there and her body then removed to somewhere else. The blood spatter pattern suggested she was struck with some object – no sign that a firearm had been used."

He continued, "As you know, a case like this stretches the resources of a small department with a small budget, serving a large, thinly-populated county with a small tax base. The sheriff did an extensive search of the property, focusing especially on a burn barrel in the back yard, but forensic examination found no human remains in the barrel and no bone fragments in the ash they removed from it. Just household trash.

"The sheriff brought in search dogs and looked for freshly disturbed earth, with no luck. They even dug up a large garbage pit on the land where Kapinski apparently had been burying tin cans, chicken guts and kitchen scraps for years. Nothing."

"So where does the case stand now?" Shane asked.

"Privately, the sheriff thinks those pigs destroyed the evidence. Of course, he's not saying that publicly, and certainly not to the family. He's reached a dead end unless someone comes forward with new information."

"What's the story on Kapinski's home here on Whidbey?"

"We did a drive-by and it's a dump, apparently much like the property in Forks, with a yard full of equipment parts, grease and oil barrels and outright garbage. He's got an old Ford Bronco sitting on blocks in the yard. The house is a modular home on several acres of land. It looks pretty neglected. Do you want us to knock on his door?"

"Yes. Let's see if we can rattle him a little. Ask where he was around the time of each murder, especially this last one. Ask if he has an alibi for any of these periods. Press him a little. I saw him on the ferry Christmas Eve, so if he lies about that, we'll know."

Shane continued, "Anything on Bob's Boatworks?"

"Bob is married and lives in Coupeville. We've got the address and contact information. He's well-regarded in the wooden boat community – something of a loner, though."

Shane filed the information in the back of his mind in case he needed to come back to it later. Bob sounded like a long shot.

As the meeting broke up, Shane asked Kat, "What do you think about all this?"

"I think there are some real lowlifes tucked away on this island."

"It's probably true of all rural communities," Shane said. "These places attract people who want to live under the radar, sometimes for good reasons and sometimes for bad. In the cities, people and their problems are packed together and you can't really hide.

"Keep in mind, the lowlifes are the ones who come to our attention as law officers. A lot of worthwhile people live on the island, too – professionals, artists, retirees from accomplished careers. They don't take much of our time. All it takes is a few of the other kind to warp one's view of humanity."

*

"Mrs. King?" asked the sheriff's deputy on the front step when Nadya opened the door in her bathrobe. Her heart sped up when she saw the uniform. In Russia, a visit from the police is bad news.

"No, I am Nadya Komanesch."

"I'm sorry to disturb you. I'm looking for Mrs. King," the deputy explained. "We were asked to do a welfare check. Is she home, or is Mr. King home?"

"Meesus King doesn't live here. Meester King is in shower."

"I can wait a few minutes to talk with him. Are you related to the family?"

"I am guest of Meester King. What family? Also, I don't understand welfare."

"I'm sorry. Let me explain," he said slowly. "A relative of Mrs. King has been trying to call her."

"This you call welfare check? In Russia we don't have."

"Mr. King told the relative his wife had gone away – he didn't know where – and he hasn't heard from her. Since then Mrs. King's phone has rung with no answer. The relative is concerned for her welfare and asked us to make contact and check on her."

"Come in. Sit down. As soon as George is out of shower, he talk with you."

She went and tapped on the bathroom door, opened it a foot, and told George about the officer. A cloud of steam and humidity poured from the opening.

When George appeared a few minutes later in his white bathrobe, he greeted the deputy warmly. George's face was flushed pink from the shower.

The deputy thought he looked composed and relaxed. George extended his hand and shook the officer's hand firmly. "George King," he said. "How may I help you?"

The deputy explained that Mrs. King's sister had called to request a welfare check on her home to make sure she's okay. The relative had been trying to reach her over the holidays without success.

"I wish I could help you," George replied. "Grace took off without saying a word and I haven't seen her since. I have suspected for some time that she had a boyfriend."

"How long ago?" the officer asked.

"In the last few days."

Nadya raised her hand to her mouth. The deputy caught the motion out of the corner of his eyes.

"Can you be more specific?"

"December 23rd, I think it was."

"What time?"

"I don't know. I was away most of the day running errands. When I got home in the afternoon and she was gone, I figured she was out shopping."

"Did she take her purse and cell phone?" the deputy asked.

"Yes, I believe so. She usually keeps them on the kitchen

counter right here."

"Was there any sign of a disturbance in the house – anything that didn't look right?"

"Not that I noticed."

"And you didn't file a missing person's report."

"Well, when it became clear she wasn't coming back, and since I was pretty sure she had run off with her boyfriend, there didn't seem much point. I'm a civil engineer and travel for periods of time on projects, so we're often going opposite directions. It was Christmas, you know, a special time for romantics." He shrugged his shoulders.

The deputy glanced at Nadya, whose mouth was open, then back at George and nodded.

"Do you have a name for this boyfriend, or a way I can get in touch with him?"

"That's not the kind of information Grace shares with me. She's been very secretive about him."

"Any idea where he works?"

"None whatsoever."

"But he lives here on the island?

"Apparently."

Can you think of anyone she might have told about this boyfriend?"

"Grace is a telecommuter. She doesn't have many acquaintances here on the island. Her friends are her coworkers in New Mexico."

"What is her work?"

"She's with a software development company called Breakout E-Solutions. Grace travels to Santa Fe sometimes for meetings with them."

"Did it cross your mind she might be the victim of foul play?"

"No, but I suppose it's possible. Knowing she has a boyfriend, I just assumed she ran off with him and it was all very romantic. I don't know how close their relationship is – maybe it's more volatile than I assumed. Are you suggesting her boyfriend might be a suspect in her disappearance?"

"I can't speculate on that. We have to look at everything," the officer replied. "In any case, I think that's all I need from you right now. Please call us if you hear from her," the deputy said, handing

George his card. "We may need to talk with you again."

"Of course. I'll do whatever I can to help."

"Oh, one last thing. Could you give me a photograph of her I can take with me?"

George reached into a frame on the mantle and removed the portrait, handing it to him.

Nadya showed the officer to the door, clicked it shut behind him. Then she turned and glared at George with her hands on her hips.

"December 23rd?" she demanded. "The day before you picked me up?"

"The marriage has been falling apart for years," George said. "I thought she was going to visit her sister over Christmas. When she cancelled that trip, I was going to ask her to check into a motel. I think her plan all along was to take off with the boyfriend. She goes away sometimes. It hasn't felt like a marriage for years."

"You lied to me."

Nadya sat down, rested her elbows on her knees, covered her head with both hands, and sobbed softly.

"Don't cry," George said. "Please don't cry. I feel terrible about misleading you, but look at it from my perspective. I've been alone for years. When I read your profile and saw what a kind and caring person you were, I knew you were the answer to my prayers."

"You mean when you saw what a simple fool I was."

"You are nobody's fool," George said. "I could tell that from the moment I met you."

Seeing the scope of George's deception, Nadya would have stormed out the door without looking back, but she had nowhere to go – and no way to get there. She was at the end of a dirt road, far from the nearest house, in the middle of a strange island, in a strange country, where they spoke a different language.

She was totally dependent on George, this man she knew less and less with each passing hour.

"I am sorry you had to hear that," George said. "That's all bullshit. Grace is out of my life. Nothing else matters but us – you and me."

Nadya stared at him. He reached for her hand, leading her across the room. "Come over and sit on the couch for a moment. I got you a little gift."

He stuck his hand into the pocket of the robe and pulled out a tiny box, tied with a ribbon. "I was going to wait a few days, but let's do this right now. Please open it," he instructed.

Nadya untied the bow carefully and raised the lid of the little box. It was a sparkling diamond engagement ring. Tears rolled down her cheeks.

"Is beautiful," she said, her emotions a welter of confusion.

George got down on one knee. "Nadya," he asked, "will you marry me?"

Calm and Bright

Captain Walker awoke to bright sunshine streaming through the curtains. She had fallen asleep again in the recliner. Tom, her brawny lover boy of a cat, had moved during the night to the sofa. When Walker stirred, he rolled onto his back, stretched about three feet, and waved his long forelegs in the air to ask for a tummy rub. Walker obliged him.

She walked to the window and studied the bay, which was covered in whitecaps but not the big swells of before. The wind had died down and the ferry would be back in service with a new captain. She popped two slices of bread into the toaster, then started the coffeemaker.

It was 9 a.m. She tried Tiff again and got no answer. She left another message, her voice more urgent this time than the last: "Tiff, give me a call. I'm worried about you."

Maybe Tiff had put her phone into silent mode and hadn't realized yet that she hadn't turned on the ringer again. Or maybe the explanation was something darker. She wished she had some other way to contact her.

The women's group was set up so that no one had a list of the members' actual names, addresses or land line numbers. Anonymity was paramount.

Whatever was happening with Tiff, at least Walker's ex-boyfriend apparently had gotten through the holidays without needing to stalk her. She hoped he had found a new girlfriend to distract him. But then again, she didn't wish this control freak on any woman.

She turned on the TV to catch the local news segment on the morning show. What she heard was unsettling.

"The Island County sheriff is asking for help identifying a Christmas Eve homicide victim whose body was found near Greenbank, on Whidbey Island. The deceased is a woman in her mid-thirties. Deputies ask you to call if you know of someone who went missing around that time."

Walker agonized. She did not have any solid reason to assume the worst, but Tiff had never failed to return a phone call before. She had been trying to reach Tiff for three days now. Something about this didn't feel right. She knew one Island County officer personally. He had responded to an emergency on the ferry a few months earlier, removing an abusive passenger who was having a psychotic episode and had threatened the crew. The officer had given her his card with his direct number.

She looked in her wallet, found the card, picked up the phone and dialed.

"Shane Lindstrom."

"This is Captain Gail Walker. You helped me with an incident on the *Kennewick* a few months ago."

"Yes, Captain. I remember it well. What can I do for you?"

Walker explained about Tiff, apologizing several times for the lack of details and evidence to back up her fears. "We don't know each other's real names, and haven't even been to each other's houses," she said.

Lindstrom assured her it was okay. "We're grasping at straws on this investigation at the moment," he said. "Any tip is helpful. We have a body but no missing persons report."

"Can you describe the person whose body you found?" Captain Walker asked.

"Five-eight, trim and fit, with short black hair."

"That, uh, roughly fits Tiff."

"I can't be much more specific because of the condition of the body."

The remark sent a shiver through Walker. "Is there any way you can trace a cell number back to address of the owner? I have her number and have tried reverse lookup online."

"It's tricky," Shane replied. "Cell numbers aren't available in public databases, but we do have some resources we can try. We'll get to work on this and let you know what we learn."

Shane looked up at Kat, who was sitting right across from him. "That's another potential lead. I think it's time to get the team together and look at everything."

*

"We have a body that was dumped by the roadside four days ago," Shane said, pacing back and forth in front of half-a-dozen deputies who had worked on various aspects of the case. "The question is, 'Why has no one missed her and reported her disappearance?'"

Silence.

"What do we have so far in tips from the public?"

"Forty-seven calls," a deputy reported. "Most are runaway teenagers from Seattle and Everett, nothing like the thirty-five-year-old woman we described in the bulletin. We have one missing woman from Everett who might fit the description, but the height is a little off."

"Follow up on that," Shane instructed.

Shane recapped the call he'd received from Captain Walker, admittedly a long shot. He pointed out that his chief suspect, Cordell Wurm, had no alibi for the period of the murder. Neither did the Greenbank logger, Zeke Kapinski, he'd seen on the ferry.

One of the deputies stepped forward. "I've got another long shot for you. I went out on a welfare check to a residence in Greenbank the other day – the George King residence. The wife's sister had been trying to reach Mrs. King for several days but got no answer."

"And?"

"The husband seems a nice-enough guy, soft spoken, an engineer and very cooperative, but the situation in that house felt odd. Mr. King was home with a Russian woman about half his age, who described herself as a guest in the home. He said he believed his wife had run off with her boyfriend Christmas Eve, and because of this, he hadn't filed a missing person's report."

Laughter.

The job does make one cynical, Shane thought. It could hardly be otherwise.

"Now he wonders if the boyfriend may have harmed her."

"It's worth a followup," Shane said, taking a sip of his coffee from a paper cup. "Give me the address. Meanwhile, we need to have a look at Kapinski's truck. I saw what looked like blood on the running board. Let's get out there again and ask him if we can look at the truck, but of course not say why. If the stain is still there, we need to hear his explanation of what it is, and collect a sample."

"Donovan," he continued, "see if you can trace this cell phone number to a name and address. If you get lucky, let me know."

Dating

George King was staring at a huge breast with pulsating purple veins. The pigtailed hippie had slid her loose peasant top off one shoulder so her baby could suckle while they talked in a Capitol Hill coffee shop in Seattle. Her nipple was enormous.

This was reality – no romance, mystery, or discovery, just the stark reality of that huge, engorged breast at the table as they sipped their lattes.

She had said over the phone that she had a young boy. "Is that a problem?" she asked.

"Not really," George said. "I like to keep an open mind when meeting people."

"Do you like birds?" she asked. "Some men don't. I have a Macaw that I let fly around the house."

That's two strikes, George thought.

Faced with the reality of what was in front of him, George just wanted to run out the door. It was the low point in a year of answering singles ads, and the memory still made him laugh, and wince.

He had learned a lesson about keeping an open mind, and screened his dates much more carefully since then. Right now he was sitting in a soundproof booth at a specialist hearing clinic in Coupeville.

"Repeat the word sidewalk," the recorded voice said into George's left ear.

"Sidewalk," George repeated.

"Repeat the word pa . . . t," the voice said more faintly, while static was being broadcast into George's right ear. This was harder. Was it paycheck? Paydirt? George wasn't quite sure what he'd heard, but took a stab.

"Pavement," George repeated.

George had been sitting in the booth for about fifteen minutes. The audiologist was just wrapping up his hearing exam.

"Okay, that completes the exam," Dr. Joyce Haycourt said. "I'll be right in. The door opened and a woman in a low-cut lab coat, open several buttons down, came in and sat down across from him, and smiled. She looked about forty. She was wearing a "Dr. Haycourt" name tag. She shook her blonde hair and wiped it away from her eyes with her hand. The move had a sexual quality.

"You have significant hearing loss in both ears at the higher frequencies," she said, looking right into his eyes. "So you are probably having some trouble with women's voices, bird calls, and such," she said.

"That's true," George agreed, playing along.

"But you scored extremely well on word recognition. This part of the test measures the brain's ability to interpret what it hears. If you have certain kinds of damage to your ears, you couldn't do that."

George couldn't help thinking how professionally and dispassionately she was conducting this exam in an office full of her colleagues, as if they had never met before. He wondered if she had successfully hidden the tailspin in her marriage from them altogether. The abrupt collapse of that relationship must be supremely embarrassing and humiliating to her.

She had scheduled this hearing test for him weeks ago, right after they'd met. Since then, he'd gotten to know Dr. Haycourt much better, to his regret. They had a one-night-stand in early October, which he hoped was now ancient history, though Joyce did not seem as ready to move on as he was. Her instability and neediness frightened him.

He had answered her personal ad. She had not identified herself as a doctor, just as a woman going through divorce who wanted to meet a professional man on Whidbey Island. They'd met for dinner in Coupeville and she had invited him back to her apartment. They'd had sex before he realized how fragile she was, and he could now see that it meant a great deal more to her than it did to him. She told him he was only the second man with whom she'd ever been intimate, her husband of eighteen years being the first and only.

She had taken to calling George at all hours and breathing heavily over the phone, which she apparently thought he would find sexy. He didn't, but was afraid it would destroy her if he said something. Dr. Haycourt told him she'd been an emotional wreck for months, drinking too much and getting stopped twice for speeding by county deputies.

That's when George realized it was her husband who had initiated the divorce. Joyce was the one being dumped, adding to her deep feelings of rejection and insecurity. It struck George that a person can be quite competent in one part of their life and entirely helpless in another.

She'd talked her way out of one of the traffic stops, but if the pattern continued, she could lose her driver's license altogether. She spent a night in jail for flunking an alcohol test, got a good lawyer, and agreed to attend counseling.

Most distressing to George, she pressed him all the time about the progress of his divorce. "These things take time," he told her.

"Don't you wish you could just snap your fingers and she'd be gone?" Joyce asked. "We should hire a hit man."

*

Dr. Haycourt was the most troublesome of George's secrets but not the only one, and it was hard to keep them all straight, so that he didn't say the wrong thing in front of the wrong person. Aside from the clingy relationship with Joyce Haycourt, George had been dating other women, too, for more than a year – mostly one date apiece, and then moving on to the next woman. After awhile the parade of possibilities becomes an addiction in itself, he concluded. He was always wondering if the next woman, just around the corner, would be the one. The singles ads had become a poverty of riches that kept him from really getting to know someone.

He'd been replying to online personals from all over Puget Sound and had grown terribly frustrated.

He kept telling himself that when the chemistry felt right, it would be with someone he never would have considered on paper. So he met the carpenter whose parents both were behind bars, the spacey Scientologist who said she was "clear," the woman with the restraining order still having sex with her ex, the mild mannered librarian, the brainy accountant, the sexy nurse, and the beleaguered divorcee with eight children.

By contrast, the Russian personals were a breath of fresh air. He found the women attractive, wholesome and domestic. He sensed they were more likely to appreciate the life they could have in the West, and not so demanding of a sugar daddy who could enable them to "have it all." The more he thought about it, the more he was intrigued with the possibilities.

One ad stood out to him in the sea of prospective women. Nadya Komanesch was beautiful and seemed well educated, high spirited, a straight-shooter and sure of what she wanted. She was looking for a kind, professional man, and George felt he fit this description. He had a lot to offer – a beautiful house on a beautiful island, a good income and a comfortable lifestyle. On a whim he wrote her a long email, and to his pleasant surprise, she answered in two hours. He was intrigued, and hooked.

Now, weeks later, she was sitting right in front of him in his house in Greenbank. Everything was hanging in the balance of how convincingly he explained his wife's disappearance. He knew he was teetering on the verge of losing Nadya.

*

"This is awfully sudden," Nadya said of his Hail Mary proposal of marriage. "We barely know each other. I need a little time to think, and you still need a divorce."

"Then while you think, let's do some sightseeing," George suggested. "Pack a bag for overnight. The next few days will be sunny, a good time to tour the area. You should see Coupeville and the historic, old Captain Whidbey Inn, and Ebey's Prairie. In fact, we could even take the ferry to Port Townsend."

As they drove north past Lagoon Point, Nadya caught glimpses of the snowy Olympic Mountains. They were so large and close, she thought they looked like pictures she'd seen of the Himalayas.

When they reached the rolling fields of Greenbank Farm, the island's narrowest point, she could see water on both sides of them. People were walking in the snowy fields, with dogs bounding ahead of them, playing. "We should get dog," she said to George. "Then we walk here."

She got her first view of another mountain range on the

opposite side, which George identified as the Cascade Mountains, the higher peaks covered in winter snow.

"You can see several volcanoes," George said, "Mount Baker, Glacier Peak, and of course Mount Rainier." It was all beautiful. She was beginning to think maybe George was right that this was heaven on Earth. She could see herself living here.

They spent some time window-shopping in the quaint village of Coupeville, including half-an-hour in the bookstore, which they loved. The owner, Meg, had many book recommendations for Nadya as a newcomer to the area.

Then they drove across Ebey's Prairie to the site of the original ferry landing on the island. George pointed out the old Ferry House where travelers stayed while they waited for the boat. "We'll come back and hike along the bluff sometime – it's the top favorite walk of everyone who lives here," George said. "But right now, let's take a look at Fort Casey and then walk aboard the ferry to Port Townsend."

Fort Casey, he explained, was one of three military installations on both sides of Admiralty Inlet, built in the 1890s to defend Puget Sound from invading navies. Today it is a state park, and part of it is a retreat center owned by Seattle Pacific University.

"Oh, look at the deer," Nadya exclaimed, pointing out a group of half-a-dozen that were munching on grass and standing around in front of the old officers' quarters.

"They're basically tame. We see them almost every time we visit the fort."

He added, "We have a few minutes. Let's get out and look around." He parked by the parade ground behind a long bunker of concrete fortifications, and they walked up on top of the bluff. The views were breathtaking from the high ground. They could see Port Townsend and the Olympic Mountains just across the water. Several people were flying kites, and George said it's a popular activity at the fort because there's usually a breeze. Nadya wanted to see the lighthouse, something they didn't have in Chelyabinsk. She thought its lines were elegant, and she tried to imagine what life must have been like for the light keepers who staffed this lonely outpost a century ago.

George pointed out Fort Flagler and Fort Worden on the far shore, the other two forts that made up the triangle of fire a century ago.

"Did they ever fight enemy ships?" Nadya asked.

"No, they never did – never fired a shot in anger. They just practiced for ships that never came."

"Is that an eagle?" she asked, pointing to a black and white bird circling overhead.

"It sure is – a Bald Eagle, our national symbol. We see them often because they nest and hunt here."

When they reached Keystone Harbor, George parked the car along the roadside. "Grab your overnight bag, Nadya," he said. "Adventure awaits us in Port Townsend."

Nadya couldn't help thinking George made her feel young again.

They bought walk-on tickets from the kiosk in the waiting room. They could see the *Kennewick* in the distance, a white speck on the blue water, coming their way. They'd be on board the boat soon.

*

At the Eagles' Inn, Shane's cell phone rang. "This is Donovan," the caller said. "I've got a name and address for that cell phone number you gave me. You're going to want to hear this."

Into the Wild

The wall of snow-capped peaks rose higher in front of them with each passing minute. Nadya stood in the ferry's forward lounge and studied the deep canyons and snowfields ahead. It seemed like this boat was carrying them to a dark and mysterious place. Miles and miles of deep forest lay ahead of them on the Olympic Peninsula, between where they were right now and the pounding surf of the Pacific beaches. She sensed those forests and mountains were unknowable even on the best day – holding a thousand secret places to disappear.

She felt George's arm graze her shoulders and slide down to her waist, drawing her hips closer. His touch was not such a shock now as it was the first time. Their bodies were getting to know each other. She wrapped her own arm around him – around this man who was both her rock of familiarity and a mystery at the same time, like those mountains. She was a long way from Chelyabinsk.

They were crossing the main shipping channel of Admiralty Inlet, George said, pointing out containerships and tugs off their bow, headed toward the open water of the Strait of Juan de Fuca.

Coming toward them was a large, fully enclosed ship, riding high. Unlike many other ships of which she'd seen pictures, this one had no containers on its deck.

"That's an odd ship," she remarked. "It doesn't seem to be carrying anything."

"It's an automobile transport," George said, "probably from Japan or Korea, with hundreds of cars inside so they aren't exposed to the weather." Nadya thought it was remarkable that Americans had so many vehicles, and had special ships to bring more from Japan and Korea. There was so much wealth.

She was surprised when a sleek, blue-and-white passenger vessel passed them moving fast, throwing a wake of water and spray into the air behind it.

"That's the Victoria Clipper, en route from Seattle to Vancouver Island," George said. "It's a twin-hulled catamaran with water-jet propulsion." He was talking like an engineer from Chelyabinsk. Water-jet propulsion sounded like something that might be manufactured in her industrial hometown, out of pipes, pumps and hoses.

As the *Kennewick* neared Port Townsend, the view changed to Victorian homes and red brick buildings. The old sea-faring town captivated her.

"This is like sailing back in time," she told George.

"You'll like the shops and restaurants when we walk around town. Whenever Whidbey Islanders are in the mood for a special meal, we just hop on the ferry for the forty-minute ride. There's an old theatre, the Rose, that is a real favorite of many. And of course all the wooden boats."

*

Captain Gail Walker stood on the bridge and watched the foot passengers go ashore. People were endlessly interesting, and you could tell a lot by how they dressed, what they carried and the way they walked.

People watching was one of the perks of her job.

Walker smiled as a middle-aged couple went up the ramp with their arms around each other, carrying small bags in their free arms. They were likely lovers on a winter getaway. They stopped as soon as they reached the over-water pier, put down their bags, and the woman pointed uptown at the buildings on pilings along the shore. The man kept his arm around her, but now he was pointing, too, explaining something. He seemed to know the town. The woman must be seeing it for the first time.

The ferries served such diverse purposes – one part vital transportation link, and another part "love boat" for those in the glow of romance.

While Walker's mind was on safety and a thousand systems aboard the boat, others like this couple were running on hormones and dreaming of the night ahead. Whatever this couple's story, she wished them a happy ending.

The last foot passengers had left the boat and the crew was now unloading vehicles. This was where accidents could happen if a deckhand gave confusing signals or a driver's attention lapsed. Walker turned her attention to watching this process closely.

*

"Holy cow," Shane said. "Talk about a break!"

He pondered the name Donovan had given him. He'd heard it just recently, but where? Kat was standing right next to him.

"Does the name Grace King mean anything to you?" he asked.

Kat looked up from her cell phone, on which she had been typing with both thumbs: *pock pock pock . . . pock . . . pock pock.*

"Wasn't she the subject of that welfare check the other day — where the door was answered by the husband's Russian girlfriend?"

"That's it."

"It appears Grace King is the mysterious 'Tiff' that Captain Walker has been trying to reach. She lives in Greenbank, about three miles from where our 'Jane Doe' was found."

"Holy cow."

"That's what I said. She and Captain Walker both belong to the same support group for women suffering from domestic abuse. But please keep that confidential. Captain Walker is pretty sensitive about people knowing."

"Do you think the husband did it?" Kat asked.

"It sure looks that way to me right now. He has a lot of explaining to do. But it's also possible someone entered the house and murdered her, such as Cordell Wurm or Zeke Kapinski, or the boyfriend Mr. King says she has. The King house is only a few hundred feet from Kapinski's compound. That's quite a coincidence. Let's get out there and see what George King has to say."

*

The King residence was dark and the drapes and mini-blinds shut when Shane and Kat pulled into the circular drive out front. The Lexus that one of the deputies had observed in the driveway earlier was gone, and the house was locked.

It struck Kat that George was incriminating himself by

disappearing just when his wife had been found murdered. How could he explain this?

Kat noticed Shane glancing around for security webcams. "No cameras that I can see," he said. "We can snoop outside as much as we like." They walked to the back and found a Dodge 4x4 with a canopy parked behind the garage. The property was tidy, as one might expect of an engineer.

"If you lived here and needed to transport a body, how would you do it?" Shane asked.

"I'd use that truck," Kat replied, nodding toward the Dodge. "Especially in snow."

"Then you'd better have a look at it," Shane suggested as he got out and headed for the shop and garage.

Kat watched Shane try the garage doors with no luck. He then cupped his hands and peered through the window into the shop, as Kat started a walk-around inspection of the vehicle.

"Grace's Honda is inside the garage," he shouted over to her.

As Shane snooped around the back of the house, she looked closely at the truck's bumpers and front end. She opened the driver's door and checked inside the cab. Then she went around to the passenger side and checked the glove box, but found no receipts or other items that drew attention to themselves. She looked in the door pockets and under the seats, but these areas were clean. At the back of the truck she opened the canopy and tailgate, and started inspecting the cargo area closely.

"I may have something here," she called to Shane.

He came over and joined her. "What does this look like to you?" Kat asked.

"Blood."

It was not a whole lot, but it left a trail right across the tailgate, as if something had been dragged out the back.

"By the way, the keys are in it," Kat said. "He must just leave them in the ignition."

Shane looked closely at the trail of blood. "He could be a hunter. There are enough hunters on this island that we need to confirm if that's human or animal blood. He pulled a plastic evidence bag from his pocket and scraped some of the dried, red substance into it."

He added, "Hard to say when he's coming back, but I think we have enough at this point to request a search warrant. I'd like to talk with Captain Walker some more, too."

Widow's Walk

Nadya stared at the elegant, Victorian home on the hill, overlooking the Port Townsend waterfront. It was ornate and stately, with wide stairs leading up to the front porch, white columns and a bay window for the dining room. The house was painted gray and white, a pleasing combination for the color of the winter sky. The roof had several peaks and a weather vane of a whale facing into the breeze.

"Beautiful!" she enthused. "But why they build porch on top of roof?"

"That's a widow's walk," he replied. A century ago this inn had been a sea captain's house. George explained the lore to her that widow's walks were built to give the wives of ship's captains a place to watch the sea for their husbands, who might go away for months at a time.

Being from a city in the interior of Russia, Nadya was not familiar with the concept.

Sometimes, George said, a sea captain's wife would continue to watch the horizon long after her husband's ship had been lost and gone to the bottom. Nadya found the story enchanting. She wondered about the woman who lived here a hundred fifty years ago, when this was a new house.

What did that woman want from her life, and did she find it in her marriage to the sea captain? Was it a lonely life or a good life, waiting for her husband to return from distant ports? How did life end for both of them?

George broke her train of thought. "Let's check in so we can get rid of these bags and leave them in the room. Then we can walk around more freely."

They climbed the steps, found the owner and signed in, then climbed the stairs to their room.

With its Victorian décor, lace curtains and frilly bed coverings, the room was everything Nadya loved. There was even a teddy bear on the bed, and a chocolate on each pillow. Sunshine streamed through the tall casement windows of their room. The view was of Port Townsend Bay. They could watch the ferry come and go to Whidbey Island.

George had chosen this luxury bed-and-breakfast, The Widow's Walk, a few blocks from the ferry landing. Nadya wondered if this was George's way of hiding out for a few days, making himself unreachable by the police or perhaps other women.

Still, Port Townsend seemed very romantic. This was such a far cry from the industrial architecture of her home. George was sweeping Nadya off her feet, and she was feeling better about him by the minute. She would like a clearer idea of what was happening with his marriage, but she would wait and bring that up when it wouldn't spoil their getaway.

As she set down her bag, George caught her in the middle of the room and gave her a long, tight hug. They kissed passionately and Nadya found herself backing up toward the bed, growing weak in the knees.

Suddenly, George stopped. "We'd better save this for later," he said, releasing his grip on her. "We'll miss the town and lose our daylight if we let ourselves get distracted right now."

"But it's such nice distraction," she remarked.

They spent the next three hours walking the cobblestone streets, arm in arm. They browsed in several galleries and shops that weren't very busy, and found the shopkeepers friendly and talkative. Everyone fawned over Nadya and her accent, and wanted to hear the story of what had brought her to Port Townsend.

"Tourism," she said. When she mentioned Chelyabinsk, some people scratched their heads and said, "That rings a bell. Why does it sound familiar?"

"Because of Chelyabinsk Event," Nadya said.

That's what they wanted to hear. "What was it like? Were you scared? Many had seen dash cam videos of the meteor that had circulated widely on social media.

George and Nadya found a quiet bistro and made small talk

74

while they had coffee. She caught George staring absently at her breast, his mind a thousand miles away. She didn't mind. She was glad George found her attractive. She had worn lacy red underwear today and a bit of her bra was showing. Maybe it was giving George ideas.

After awhile, they went next door and listened to a jazz trio.

Much of the time they just window-shopped. When they grew tired of that, they had a leisurely dinner at an airy seafood restaurant by the marina. Nadya was glad she had taken a chance and made the long journey from Russia to meet George.

Nadya was pretty sure George had some secrets, perhaps even dark ones. Whatever they were, Nadya felt a comfortable connection with him that seemed real. She hoped he was ready to leave his past behind, whatever it was, and build a future with her. But one thing puzzled her.

"Do they have Costco here?" Nadya asked. "We have walked all over this town. Vanya say, 'When you get to America, go to Costco.' I do not see Costco."

"Let me explain some things to you about small towns and what makes them so charming," George replied. "People in some of these quaint, historic towns don't want the big box stores like Costco, Walmart and Home Depot, nor fast food like McDonalds. They destroy the small-town character."

"They don't want Costco?" she asked. "Where they shop?"

"Next time we'll bring the car and drive to Sequim," George said. "It's a big retirement community. They have Costco there."

"Sequim?" Nadya asked, mimicking George's pronunciation of skwim. "What kind of name is that?"

"It's a Native American word, from the Klallam language."

"And it means what, Costco?"

George laughed. "They used to translate it as quiet waters. A few years ago they decided it really meant a place for going to shoot. The valley there has large waterfowl and elk populations."

"I'll never learn the language here," Nadya said. "Too many Native names on top of all the English ones."

"We haven't even gotten to the good ones yet – Puyallup, Swinomish, Muckleshoot, Tulalip . . ."

"Stop, stop!"

Nadya's thoughts already had moved on. She was eager to get

back to George's house in Greenbank. She was looking forward to boxing up some of his wife's personal possessions and helping him redecorate. That would help him forget the past.

Captain Walker

Captain Gail Walker stared at her coffee cup, which she was holding in both hands, as rain lashed at the windows of Callen's Café, at the Keystone Ferry Landing. It was a classic winter day of rain and wind on the west side of the island, which was fully exposed to storms off the Strait of Juan de Fuca. The captain found the warm café and the weather comforting. She was off duty today and had made the crossing to Whidbey Island as a passenger. This seventy-year-old café was one of the coziest places she knew.

"Wow," Captain Walker said. "I just had no idea Tiff was from Whidbey Island."

"Apparently, that's how she wanted it," Shane said. "She didn't want to run into anyone she knew, so she joined a Port Townsend women's group. She was covering her tracks from George and anyone else who might be curious about her secrets."

Shane and Kat had been waiting inside the terminal building when Captain Walker came up the loading ramp from the ferry, in her foul-weather gear. They were not dressed to stand outside in this gale, but Shane gave Kat his umbrella. It promptly blew inside out with a *whap*.

At the café, Captain Walker hung up her raincoat. She was wearing black wool slacks and a blue-and-black striped sweater. Even in casual attire she maintained a smart, commanding image.

"It's good to see you again," Shane greeted her. "This is my friend, Kat Brown, who is studying criminal justice and helping me this week." The women shook hands.

They had chosen a quiet corner table and ordered coffee and toasted bagels with cream cheese. The waitress turned three cups right side up and retrieved a coffee carafe from the warming plate nearby to fill them. She left a small pitcher on the table with cream. A few moments later their bagels arrived.

Shane filled in Captain Walker on what he knew at this point. Tiff's real name was Grace King. She lived in Greenbank and worked for an out-of-state software development company. She tele-commuted part of the time, in addition to traveling to New Mexico to meet with her colleagues.

He said Grace's sister had been trying to call her over the holidays, without success. She finally called the sheriff's department and asked for a welfare check. A deputy went to the house and was met at the door by a Russian woman, Nadya Komanesch, who identified herself as a friend of the family.

"Oh for crying out loud!" Walker exclaimed, looking up at the ceiling. "He's been playing the international personals."

"So it appears."

When the deputy performed the welfare check, he found George King relaxed and cooperative. He denied any knowledge of his wife's whereabouts. He had last seen her early in the day, December 23rd. Shane said George explained she had a boyfriend and he assumed she had run off with him, or possibly that the boyfriend had kidnapped her.

Coincidentally, the King residence was very close to the home of a person of interest whose first wife disappeared mysteriously a couple of years ago.

"So," Shane said, "what I want to know is whether Grace, or Tiff, ever mentioned the neighbor to you, or a boyfriend."

"Never. Maybe she had one, but what she talked about was how miserable she was – that she and her husband barely talked to each other anymore. She said he traveled quite a bit for his work, and when he was away everything was fine. But when he was home, they argued and fought."

"Did he harm her?"

"Not so much physically as psychologically. They got into terrible shouting matches. Her husband was a womanizer and she said he detested her. But she said something curious that she never explained. She said, 'I've gotten myself into a real mess and I'm about to do something that will blow the lid off everything.'"

"She never gave you any more clues about what it was?"

"No, she didn't seem to want to go into details. I wondered if she was referring to her husband or possibly some other man. Do you think she's okay?"

"We don't know. No one was home when Kat and I went to the house, but there were some disturbing signs we want to ask George about. Did Grace say anything else about her husband that might help us? We're trying to form a picture of who she was – what she wanted from life. Do you know much about her childhood and family?"

"I think she grew up in the Seattle area. She was a typical Northwest native, into hiking and gardening. She was very smart and had a lot of interests. When she talked about her husband, I found myself wondering why she had married him. But we all do things that, in hindsight, make no sense."

Shane and Kat were silent, giving Walker a chance to collect her thoughts.

Walker studied her coffee cup. "I'm trying to think. I guess the big thing was that her husband had a roving eye, and the more buxom the women were, the better. Even early in their marriage, he was always staring at other women. It became an issue between them – one of many. Grace said he wanted a wife to cook and clean for him, and that wasn't who she was. She loved having a career as a professional."

"I appreciate you meeting with us," Shane said. "You've given us a better sense of what was going on in that house. Before you go, I wanted to ask how you're doing with your own situation. I know you've had some problems with your ex-boyfriend. Has that settled down any?"

"Apparently," Walker said. "I was worried he might show up over Christmas but he didn't. Maybe he's finally moving on."

"I hope so," Shane said. "Call me if there's anything I can do. I'm in close touch with Jefferson County authorities."

They said their goodbyes and Walker headed back to the ferry terminal.

*

Shane and Kat got into their car and sat there a moment, each lost in their own thoughts. The windshield was bleary from the rain. Tapping at the window startled Shane and he looked up. It was

Captain Walker. Shane rolled down the glass.

"I thought of something else you might want to know about Grace. She seemed very involved with her church. Faith was obviously important to her, maybe even more so in light of her personal problems. She mentioned it several times and seemed to be getting more involved with her church. I know she was struggling with something, but she didn't tell me what it was."

"Do you know the name of her church?"

"I'm afraid not. She said it was quite large and high profile in the community."

"I appreciate knowing. If we get a chance, we'll track it down." Shane rolled up his window and Walker headed back toward the harbor again.

*

"So now what?" Kat asked.

"We search the King residence. I would prefer to execute the search warrant when George King is home, but legally, we can go ahead even if he isn't. I don't want to wait any longer. We'll leave paperwork in the house explaining to him that we entered with a warrant."

At the King residence, as they expected, no one was home. Shane knelt by the front door and inserted a lock pick into the dead bolt. "We could force open the door, but I'd rather not damage someone's property if we can avoid it," he said.

"This is a pin-tumbler lock," he explained to Kat. "You may want to study up on lock picking when you go into police work. What I'm doing right now is raking it," he said as he rapidly inserted and removed the pick many times. "It's a fast method to reset the tumblers into the open position. It's not the only way to pick a lock like this. Different locksmiths have different favorites when it comes to picks."

Within seconds he switched to a different tool, a "hook," he called it. He inserted and turned it with light pressure from one finger. He could tell Kat was impressed with his patience. The bolt retracted smoothly and Shane pushed open the door.

"That's like magic," Kat said.

"Tool of the trade. After awhile you develop a feel for this stuff. No rushing or forcing."

Kat and Shane, accompanied by two other deputies, entered the house. One of the deputies, a tech expert, headed directly for the den and began assessing the two computers, checking to see if they were password-protected. Shane was hoping to get into Grace King's email, and also look for a record of George King's correspondence with the Russian woman.

The other deputy began a systematic search, room by room, for the murder weapon or any other evidence that could help them.

Shane and Kat headed for the bedroom with a spray bottle of luminol and a black light. Shane explained that luminol reacts with the iron in hemoglobin, to detect trace amounts of blood. He sprayed the wall and floor and then switched on the black light. Both areas lit up blue. Before the luminescence faded, he pulled out his cell phone and snapped several pictures that showed big blotches of bright reflections.

"The wall and floor have been scrubbed hastily," Shane said, "most likely with bleach, but both areas were splattered with blood. It looks like this is where Grace King was murdered – right here on this bed.

"Now, let's look at the shop and garage. If George transported the body in his truck, he probably removed it from the house through the garage."

The other deputy poked his head into the room. "Finding some pretty racy underwear," he said. "The labels aren't in English. Russian, it looks like."

"Probably to be expected," Shane replied.

The door to the garage was locked, but Shane's pick opened it easily. He switched on the light and his eye immediately went to a large stain on the floor.

"I think we hit the jackpot here," he said to Kat. "George didn't have time to clean this up, so he just locked the door till he could come back later. This must be where he rolled the body into a bundle with the rug. Unless it's from a deer. But to hunt deer in December, he'd have to be using either a muzzleloader or a bow, and I haven't seen either one in this house."

"He must have backed the truck up to the garage and loaded the body right here," Kat said.

"I think we can wrap things up here and let the other officers close up the house when they finish," Shane said. "How are you coming with the computers?" he asked the deputy who was looking at them.

"We'll need to break the passwords," he said. "It shouldn't be too hard but I think we'll pack them up and continue this back at the office."

"Kat and I are going to head out," Shane said, reaching for the doorknob. Kat was just behind him.

"Just a minute. I want to check something," Kat said, drifting toward the forest edge. Shane waited till she finished looking around and came back.

"Did you know there's a trail over there, at the edge of the landscaping?" she called out to him.

"Interesting."

"Aren't you curious?"

"Oh, a little, but why are you so interested in trails? What does it have to do with our investigation?"

"Humor me," Kat said. "You know I lived on the run for several years, relying on trails in both the winter and summer. There's always a reason for them. So I like to know what it is."

Shane crossed the yard and joined Kat where she was standing.

"I don't see any trail," he said.

"No, and you wouldn't if the person who made it was trying to conceal that it was here. But when you get back through the brush a few feet, then it becomes obvious. For one thing, I notice the snow on this one is all packed down from walking," she said, pointing to a trampled area up ahead. "Someone in boots has been standing right at the edge of the trees, because there's a large area that's compacted. Want to see where it goes?"

She led Shane to the spot. He pulled a plastic glove over his hand and bent down to retrieve several cigarette butts, which he placed in a plastic evidence bag.

"We've come this far," he said. "Let's have a look at where this goes."

"Snow is wonderful because you can reconstruct the whole history of who has passed a certain way," Kat said, now breathless. "We've got a nice boot print here," she said, bending down. She laid down a ballpoint pen next to it for scale, and snapped several pictures with her iPhone.

They followed the footprints in the snow for several hundred feet till the trail opened into a junky clearing with a modular home and a logging truck parked out front. "Zeke's Wildcat Logging," said the stenciling on the door. There was also an old Dodge 4x4 pickup with an aluminum canopy.

"Holy cow!" Shane exclaimed. "Holy cow! Zeke Kapinski is one of our suspects – granted, a long shot."

"My sentiments exactly," Kat said. "This is a super shortcut through the trees between the two houses. And someone's been going back and forth. So we've got one suspect living right next door to another suspect, and now nothing is quite as open-and-shut as it seemed a few minutes ago."

"You love this work, don't you?" Shane asked. "I do, too. And you get an 'A plus' today."

Loose Ends

Elizabeth was just pulling a hot baking dish of lasagna from the oven when Shane and Kat got home.

"How did it go today?" Elizabeth asked.

"Good," Shane replied.

"Really good," Kat clarified, smiling broadly. "And that lasagna smells wonderful, too."

"So which was it?" Elizabeth asked, reaching into the refrigerator for a large bowl of organic salad greens and setting it on the table along with table settings for three. "A good day or a really good day?"

"We served a warrant on George King but no one was home, so we entered and searched the house and property anyway. Kat is feeling cocky because she discovered a tantalizing clue I was all set to overlook," Shane said. "Do not underestimate her. It turns out, two of our suspects live right next to each other and there's a short trail through the woods between their houses. Kat found the trail and turned our whole investigation on its ear."

"Way to go!" Elizabeth exclaimed.

"Yes, and she gathered some forensic evidence. It raises all kinds of bedeviling questions," Shane said. "This case is going in directions I never foresaw. I really thought we would trace the murder to Cordell Wurm, but everything points elsewhere."

He continued, "If George King is suspect number one, then Zeke Kapinski is number two. It appears very likely Kapinski murdered his wife a couple of years ago when he lived on the peninsula, but the body was never found and the sheriff could never pin it on him."

"He's a little smarter than he lets on," Kat said. "And cunning as a coyote. I'd be nervous having him next door if I knew what we're finding out about him."

*

Elizabeth curled up by the wood stove with a glass of wine while Shane pulled dishes from the soapy water, rinsed them and handed them to Kat to dry and put away. He saved the lasagna pan for last and traded his sponge for a scouring pad. A little extra scrubbing got it clean. The two of them had just finished the dishes, drained the sink and hung up the dish towels to dry when Shane's cell phone rang. Shane answered with wet hands, wiping first one, then the other, on his pants as he listened. It was the deputy who'd been studying the two computers

Kat handed him a towel too late.

"If Grace King had a boyfriend, there's no sign of it on her computer," the deputy said. "Nothing in her email. Maybe they communicated by texting, but in any case I couldn't find any trace of him."

"What about George?" Shane asked.

"That's a different story. He doesn't clear his web history cache very often. I checked and he's made many visits to a dating website that specializes in introductions to Russian women. Also, there are dozens of long, amorous emails to and from a Nadya Komanesch in Chelyabinsk."

"Chelyabinsk?" Shane asked.

"It's an industrial city near the Ural Mountains. Famous for the Chelyabinsk Event of 2013."

"I'm a little hazy on that particular event."

"I had to look it up. It was a meteor as large as a six-story building that exploded over the city."

"In any case it's obvious he had a girlfriend-in-the-making booked into the home for Christmas Eve, and would have wanted his wife out of the way. We just don't know how badly. The deputy who went to the house and met Nadya commented she was pretty well endowed."

"On top of everything else, George and Nadya are nowhere to be found, now," Shane said. "I don't know if they're gone on some innocent getaway or if they're on the run. We need to keep a close watch on that house in case they turn up again."

Shane thanked the deputy and ended the call.

"What's next?" Kat asked.

"I'm thinking we should pay a visit to Zeke Kapinski."

"I think so, too. If all George King did was get himself a Russian girlfriend, that isn't against the law, is it?"

"No, he's just colossally inept at managing his personal life. In the big scheme of things, it doesn't make him a murderer. But his neighbor, Zeke Kapinski, may already have some experience with that."

*

Shane and Kat pulled into Zeke Kapinski's yard at 8 a.m. Shane wanted to catch him at home before he left for a day of logging somewhere. The shady yard was still full of snow and tire ruts. White smoke was pouring from the chimney and swirling around the clearing. Shane could tell Kapinski had just lit a fire in the woodstove and the pipe was still cold.

Shane rapped on the door. "Sheriff's Department," he called out.

He heard a fit of coughing on the other side. The door opened and Kapinski stood there in his T-shirt and boxer shorts, with an unlit cigarette dangling from his mouth. A large bandage was taped to his forearm. He reached up and removed the cigarette from his lips. "Damn, it's cold," he said.

"Detective Shane Lindstrom," Shane said, showing Kapinski his credentials. "Go find some pants and get decent, would you?" Shane ordered. "My associate here is a woman."

"One moment," Kapinski said, closing the door.

Shane knew moments like this could be lethal if a suspect felt cornered. He didn't think Kapinski would come out shooting, but one never knows. "Keep your distance from me till we know his intentions," he said to Kat. Inside the pocket of his coat, Shane had his hand on his Glock. "God, that place reeks."

A moment later Kapinski opened the door again, this time wearing some greasy blue jeans, and with both hands in view. Shane hadn't seen him before without his Stihl baseball cap. He was bald. But his white beard flowed halfway down his chest. He wasn't very tall, not much over five feet, and Shane thought he looked like a character from Snow White and the Seven Dwarfs – Bashful, Grumpy or Dopey. He came across as charmingly goofy, but was perhaps a good deal more dangerous.

"Come in," Kapinski beckoned. "Sorry about the condition of the place. I wasn't expecting callers." He brushed some Cheetos and food wrappers off the sofa so they could sit. "To what do I owe this early-morning pleasure?"

"Something happen to your arm?" Shane asked, pointing to the bandage."

"That? A chain got away from me. Bled like a son-of-a-bitch."

"We need to ask you some questions. You're a neighbor of George King, I understand."

"That might be a stretch of the word neighbor," he replied. "I've never met the guy. His place is a good, oh, quarter mile down the road."

"There's a shorter way," Shane remarked.

"I don't follow," Kapinski said, making a show of confusion.

"Through the woods. It's just a few hundred feet."

"Maybe. I don't know."

"Gosh, you must know, Mr. Kapinski, because there's a nice trail and the snow is packed down all the way from Mr. King's house to yours."

"It is?"

"That's right. And we photographed a boot print that I'll bet matches those boots of yours sitting by the door." Shane pointed at a pair of well-worn boots.

"Okay. Look. I didn't want to make too much of that trail because it would just raise more questions. I might have been over that way hunting deer."

"With what?"

"With my trusty old muzzleloader; it's black powder season," King said, smiling and pointing at an antique rifle hanging over the sofa. "One shot. That's all you get. I might have gotten over on George King's side of the line," he said, laughing till he went into a fit of coughing. "I've got to give up the fags."

"What brand do you smoke?" Shane asked.

"Camels. Foul things."

"We found quite a pile of Camel cigarette butts right next to

George King's house. What's that all about?"

Kapinski went silent and looked down at his feet. "This is hard with the girl sitting here."

"She's a big girl," Shane said.

"Look, I get why you're here. I'm not proud of this. I don't have a regular woman in my life and I get lonely, so yes, I do go next door sometimes and watch – you know – just watch them having a normal life. Is that so wrong?" Then he added quickly, "It's not right, I know."

"Are you sure that's all you do? Because I'm pretty sure your interest goes way beyond that. Also, I understand you were married when you lived on the peninsula but your wife disappeared without a trace."

"That's true. It was tragic," Kapinski said. "They never caught the guy who did it," he remarked.

Shane and Kat looked at each other and said nothing.

"Did what?"

"Murdered her, I suppose."

"Do you know Mrs. King?"

He scratched his chin through his beard and took a moment to answer. "Not really. Just from a distance, looking, you know."

"Do you have feelings for her?"

"Normal feelings. Just the normal feelings a man has for a good-looking woman. I don't think Mr. King was very good to her."

"You speak of her in the past tense."

"Slip of the tongue. I assume she's gone and Mr. King has a new girlfriend now."

"Have you observed the Kings fighting?"

"I've seen them argue when I was watching from the edge of their property. It got pretty loud. I didn't see him lay a hand on her."

"Did you see what time Mr. King left Christmas Eve?"

"He didn't leave. He was already gone."

"What do you mean?"

"He didn't come home the night of December 23rd. I didn't see him at all on Christmas Eve until nighttime, when he showed up with the other woman. Why do you ask?"

"Because we're trying to reconstruct a timeline for some events that happened next door, and you're the only witness we have."

"Yes, I saw the woman. She was a looker, you know what I

mean?" he asked, giving Shane a wink.

"I understand Mrs. King wasn't home when George arrived with the other woman. Do you know where she is?"

Kapinski went silent. "No comment. I think I should have a lawyer."

"We're not arresting or charging you," Shane said, "just having a conversation."

"I think I've said enough. I don't know where you're going with this."

Cell Phone

On a stretch of roadside near Greenbank, eighty-three-year-old Rudolph Vaughn was walking stiffly. He had neuropathy in both feet from compressed disks in his back, which caused him to wobble off balance at times. Unsteady as he was, he calculated it was better to walk every day than give into sedentary habits. The iPhone in his pocket tracked his steps, and today he'd racked up 8,216 so far.

This was more than he got most days riding around in a Citizen's Patrol car, doing vacation checks on empty homes and serving as extra eyes and ears for the sheriff's department. He was carrying a litter bag and picking up beer cans and food wrappers as he went, not expecting them to be of any value in the active murder investigation, but because he hated litter and didn't want to overlook something important, either. The snow was mostly gone now.

Vaughn enjoyed his role with the Citizen's Patrol. It got him out of the house and gave him a sense that he still had something to contribute to the world, other than becoming decrepit and waiting to die.

The sheriff's department had identified the search area as extending from the ground at his feet out to a distance of ten yards, which they judged was about as far as someone could throw a cell phone from the driver's window of a vehicle, assuming the phone was even there at all. One thing was sure – there were lots of beer cans and candy wrappers in this world.

Vaughn was just about to cross the road and double back to his car on the opposite shoulder when his eye caught the glint of something in a patch of snow about thirty feet away. In fact the sun was reflecting off it brightly, as if it were a mirror. He wobbled across the uneven ground, nearly losing his balance twice when he stepped into holes. When he finally reached the spot, he knew he was looking at a needle in a haystack – a shiny, bright iPhone.

*

Finished for now with Zeke Kapinski, Kat and Shane got into their car and clicked their seatbelts across their laps. Shane was just reaching for the ignition button when Kat brought up what was already on his mind.

"If Kapinski is telling the truth, Mrs. King was home alone the night of the 23rd and all day on Christmas Eve, up until the time somebody killed her. If the killer entered the house the morning of December 24th while she was sleeping, he could have killed her in the way the coroner suggested, from overhead, before she could even wake up and defend herself."

"Which raises the question, where did George spend the night of December 23rd?" Shane asked. "Was he with yet another woman? Did he use that time to kill his wife and remove her body? Or did someone else get into the house and kill her?"

"Such as his next-door neighbor, Zeke Kapinski," Kat suggested.

"Or my old friend, Cordell Wurm."

Kat and Shane were just driving back from Kapinski's house when Shane's phone rang.

"One of our citizen's patrol volunteers found her cell phone," Donovan reported. "With the snow starting to melt, he searched the roadside. It was in the brush about a quarter mile from where we found the body. We're going over it now. Probably would have missed it except that the sun was reflecting off the aluminum case just right. The old geezer who found it thought it was a coke can at first."

"Any sign of her purse?"

"We think so. He found one near the phone that was missing the wallet and all identifying papers and credit cards, but had the usual items otherwise – comb, hairbrush, lipstick and such."

"I'm on my way in to look at that phone," Shane said, ending the call and looking over at Kat. "This is big. It will either confirm or upend our assumptions about a boyfriend and tell us who she was talking to at the end of her life."

"Maybe while we wait for that, we should try to find out more about who Grace and George were as people," Kat suggested. "You mentioned Grace had a sister in Montana. Maybe she could fill in some details. As for George, did he have any family?"

"That's a good question. His parents were deceased but I don't know about siblings or ex wives."

Grace's sister, Jackie Lyons, already had been in touch with the sheriff's department since she initiated the welfare check. Shane called her back at that number.

He filled her in on developments in the case. She already knew that a body had been found that was tentatively identified as Grace, but not that some of her personal effects had been recovered nearby.

She confirmed that Grace had been unhappy for years, and had dealt with it by consuming herself more and more in her work for the Santa Fe software firm. She and George had managed their relationship mostly by avoiding each other – staying busy with travel for their separate jobs. Things often got tense when they were together at home.

"Was she afraid for her safety?" Shane asked.

"I think so," Jackie said. "She said George had quite a temper and was hiding something. Of course, Grace had secrets of her own – we all do. I sometimes felt she was sheltering me from the truth of how bad things were, maybe because she didn't want to burden me with her problems. She suspected George was seeing other women."

"Did she ever mention a boyfriend of her own?"

"She had friends. Most were associates in the software firm, but she did mention someone local named David."

"In what way?"

"Oh, we'd be talking and she'd say, 'I need to go because I think my friend David is trying to reach me,' things like that. She never called him a boyfriend, but when I read between the lines, I think he was. One time she said, 'I'm meeting my friend David for dinner.'"

"You've been very helpful," Shane said. "I'll keep you advised as we learn more."

"Is George your chief suspect?"

"We're certainly looking at him," Shane said, "but there are complicating factors that may point to others. So at this stage we're still putting together all the evidence and looking at how it adds up.

I'm quite confident we're going to solve this case and get a conviction."

Shane ended the call, then got on his laptop and went to LinkedIn. He found George's curriculum vitae listing all the schools where he received his education, and some of his more noteworthy projects in recent years – water treatment plants, sewage lagoons, storm water systems. It listed several personal references. Shane chose one from the recent past who was listed as a hunting partner, and dialed the number, and introduced himself.

"I'm looking at George King's LinkedIn page and he lists you as a hunting partner and a character reference," Shane began.

"Oh, that's right. He said he was naming me as a reference. No one has ever called before."

"Do you know him fairly well?"

"Fairly well. We've hunted together several times, and you know how it goes, you get to talking because there are long periods of boredom. Is there some problem?" the guy asked. "He's a friend and I don't want to speak against him."

"We're working on a case in which Mr. King may be involved and wanted to talk with someone who knows him away from the job. I'm sorry I can't be more specific at this time. I hope you'll be honest and candid."

"Sure. I'll be glad to help as much as I can."

"Can you tell me what he is like as a friend?"

"Pleasant. Good natured. I've always found him quite helpful."

"So his temperament, as far as you've seen, is calm and steady?"

"Yes. If anything I'd say it's almost subdued, with maybe a touch of sadness sometimes."

"Sadness? That's interesting."

"Well I suppose no one has a perfect life," the friend acknowledged. "I've had the feeling things never worked out for George in the romance department. He seems to have a lot weighing on his mind."

"Did you ever get a sense of what that is?"

"I'd say his marriage is the big one. It really sounds like he and his wife don't get along. He said a couple years after they got married, she lost all interest in sex."

"Has he ever mentioned girlfriends?"

"Now you're asking me to betray a confidence. Yes, he talked about girlfriends. I think he has some insecurities about women. He was always trying to meet new women and get them to validate him somehow. Last time I saw him, he was doing something online with an international dating site."

"Do you think he's capable of violence?"

"George? Oh no. Not at all. Not George."

Shane thanked the friend for his help and said he'd call again if there was anything else.

*

In Port Townsend, Nadya felt the moment had come to raise uncomfortable questions. George seemed in no hurry to go back to the island. In fact they'd gone out and bought extra clothes to extend their stay.

"George, I'm having wonderful time and I think you are lovely man, but I need help understanding some things."

She noticed him grimace. She could tell he knew what was coming.

"What is going on with your wife? You told that policeman you last saw her December 23rd, the day before you pick me up, yet you led me to believe you were separated and hadn't seen her in a long time."

"I was afraid of losing you," he replied. "If I told you she was still living in the house, I didn't think you would make the trip. More than anything in the world I wanted to meet you and begin a new life. You were my one shot at something better. I was sure I could get her out of the way so she wouldn't be around when you visited."

"Well, if you expect to begin new life with me, it must be based on honesty. Your wife seems to have been in the house until just before I arrive, which is remarkable coincidence, and you don't seem very curious about her disappearance. You also don't seem in hurry to get back home and help police."

"I told you, she had a boyfriend. I think she ran off with him. Or possibly he kidnapped her. Either way, it's out of my control."

"If she is dead, you should want to know why, and feel compassion for her. I thought I was going to die once," Nadya said. "I can't describe how it feels, knowing you have only minutes, maybe seconds, to live."

"When was that?" George asked.

"When meteor came. It was brighter than the sun. We did not know what it was, but assumed it was the beginning of nuclear war. Your country had done what we always feared – sent nuclear missiles and caught us in a first strike. What else could we think?"

"It must have been terrifying," George allowed.

"When it exploded, it showered the earth with debris, but the worst was all the windows breaking and falling to the street. Bricks fell. People were hurt – killed. If the blast didn't kill us, we thought radiation would."

"Why are you telling me this?"

"Because I don't know what happened to your wife, but I know what it's like to think you are going to die. I don't want to live in fear that I could be killed like she was."

"That could never happen."

"Let me tell you about growing up," she began, relating the story of her family in Chelyabinsk. Nadya recounted a carefree childhood, playing with friends. Her parents loved and provided for her, even though they had little extra for themselves. "When you are little girl, little princess, the future is bright and beautiful. I studied hard in school, to make something of myself."

But the older she got, the more clearly she saw the future for her was not so beautiful as it seems to a child's eyes. She would work as a hotel maid, or in the same factories where her parents and grandparents had grown old and stooped, barely scraping by. Her girlfriends married dispirited men who drank themselves numb and abused their wives.

"I make decision I will seek better life for myself in West, and that's why I sign up for international dating site. I take huge risk," she said. "I am not stupid or foolish girl. I know what I want, and it is love, and truth. Do you know what you want? If it is not a wife with whom to share the rest of your years, how can I be sure I won't wind up like Grace?"

George sat on the edge of the bed, silent and stunned.

*

Shane and Kat sat at Shane's desk in the sheriff's department.

Kat was twirling a pen on the desk, feeling the need to make something happen.

Grace's cell phone was on the desk in front of them. Shane explained the department and several other agencies on the island shared a cell phone hacking tool called GrayKey, which had enabled them to discover Grace's password and get into her phone. "Apple keeps improving security on its iPhones, but as fast as they do it, hackers and security researchers find new ways to get around it," Shane said. "This is the tool law enforcement agencies are using now."

He started scrolling through Grace's apps.

"Bingo!" he said. "This is what I wanted to find."

"What?"

"It's the cell phone app for Grace and George's bed. It's one of those high-tech, adjustable beds that gives you an electronic report every day on how well you slept." Shane tapped on the screen to open a display.

"You can't be serious," Kat said, rolling her eyes.

"I am. Take a look at this," Shane said, turning the phone so Kat could see the display.

"Now we know exactly the moment Grace died – 6:02 a.m. – and also what time the killer removed her body from the bed – 4:42 pm, December 24th.

"How do you know that?"

Shane pointed to a green bar on the display. "This is a graph of Grace's night's sleep. It shows she got into the bed at 11:23 pm, December 23, and fell asleep ten minutes later. She slept fairly soundly until 6:02 a.m., when the app recorded a short period of restlessness. The app uses a gold color for that, and red for 'bed exits.'

"I think the killer entered the house early on the morning of the 24th and murdered Grace before she woke up. What the bed interpreted as restlessness at 6:02 a.m. was the movement of her body as the killer bludgeoned her. After she was dead, the bar turned gray, meaning she was still in bed but neither asleep nor restless, just lying there. So the killer left her body lying on the bed for much of the day, maybe while he did some cleaning and figured out how he was going to dispose of it. At 4:42 pm, the app finally showed a "bed exit" in red, which would be the killer removing the weight of Grace's body from the bed."

"That's diabolical," Kat said.

"Technology," Shane said. "Nobody can keep secrets any more."

Shane continued, "Grace's sister mentioned someone named David as a possible friend. We've got Grace's cell phone now and we've got texts and a phone number for David, so how about we give him a call on Grace's phone?"

Kat nodded.

Shane dialed and waited as it rang several times. "Grace?" came the answer. "Oh thank god."

"David?" Shane asked. "Is this David?"

"Who's calling?" he asked. "I don't give out this number."

"This is Detective Shane Lindstrom with the Island County Sheriff's Department."

"Is this about Grace? I saw the caller ID and assumed it was her. Is she ok?"

"You tell me."

David explained he'd tried to call Grace several times over the last few days, with the calls all going to voice mail. He had seen the news bulletin about a woman's body found near Greenbank and was worried it was her.

"I'm sorry to say we believe it is her," Shane said, "but we don't have positive ID yet."

"Do you have a suspect?"

"Several," Shane replied. "We're winnowing them down." Shane asked David for his full name and address, which turned out to be in Coupeville, a fifteen-minute drive from Grace's home, and a two-block walk from the sheriff's office. "We'd like you to come into the office so we can sit down and talk some more."

"Of course," David said. "Just understand that Grace was very afraid of George. I was trying to help her get away from him before something happened. I think she had other fears, too. I don't know what they all were."

After Shane hung up, he turned to Kat. "So now we know George was telling the truth; there really was a boyfriend right here on the island."

"Do you think David could have killed her?"

"No, my gut tells me he didn't. He sounded genuinely

surprised and relieved when I called him on Grace's phone. He thought he was getting a call from her. Said he had been worried for days. I believe him."

Kat stared at Shane, perhaps not quite as trusting as he was of David.

Shane added, "I noticed he brought up George as a threat to Grace's safety, as others have done, either because it's true or because he wanted to deflect suspicion away from himself.

"Well, here's a scenario for you," Kat said. "Imagine George announced to Grace he was going to spend the 23rd with a girlfriend. Grace called David and invited him over to the house for a romantic night alone.

"At some point during the evening she may have had second thoughts about the relationship and told him it was over – she couldn't do it anymore. They argued. After everything he had tried to do for her, he felt betrayed. The argument grew more heated. If he couldn't have her, nobody could. Maybe he left to go home, and Grace went to bed, but David came back toward morning and let himself in. He went and got a hammer from the shop, came into her room and hit her.

"Realizing what he'd done and how it looked, he set about dumping the body and framing George," Kat suggested.

"He'd have to be an awfully good actor to have answered the telephone the way he did," Shane said.

"Maybe he knew this day was coming – that sooner or later he'd get a call from an investigator and he would need to be on his best game. But setting David aside for a moment, what about Zeke?" Kat asked. "What do you make of his story?"

"Up to a point it rings true," Shane said, "but he's holding something back. He was obsessed with Grace and George. Watching that house the way he did from the edge of the clearing, he knew who was home and who wasn't. George was away the night of December 23rd. Kapinski had the opportunity to enter the house toward morning of December 24th and kill Grace King. He had time to do some cleanup before leaving for the peninsula to pick up a load of logs, establishing an alibi. When he returned later in the day, he could see George hadn't been home, so removed her body through the garage, into George's truck. That would have put him on the same ferry as me.

"George left the keys in his truck," Shane added. "When he came home later with Nadya, his mind was not on looking in his shop or the back of his own truck."

"Would anyone really go to the trouble of cleaning up the murder scene in someone else's house?" Kat asked.

"I don't know but it's possible. They might if they wanted to eliminate any evidence of their involvement, and cast suspicion on the husband. It's just possible."

Funds Transfer

The two men leaned over opposite sides of the desk in the dimly lit real estate office, looking at a ledger. The receptionist had left for the evening and they were alone in the quiet building.

"I'm just going to ask you straight out, does this have anything to do with Grace King?" asked the shorter, balding man.

"Absolutely not," replied the taller man with luxuriant black hair.

"You've got her under control?"

"Yes. She won't be a problem."

"I keep going over the numbers and they're not adding up," the balding man said, scratching his head. "We're going to get some questions from the board. We show almost nothing in cash, currency, in the collection plate. The discrepancy is so great from normal patterns it's going to call attention to itself. Our attendance in November was huge and the cash collection should be huge as well."

The taller man stood up, ramrod straight, and smiled. "You're right. Cash offerings were outstanding. I took the opportunity to deposit some funds into a special account for a project that I'd rather not disclose just yet, but trust me, it's all part of the Lord's work and he is going to bless our efforts."

Cash was something Pastor Tom especially loved about the Lord's work. Many members of the congregation on a Sunday simply reached into their billfolds for a twenty-dollar bill and dropped it into the plate. All the loose cash didn't show up in formal pledges. Those were accounted for separately, and usually came in the form of checks in collection envelopes labeled with the giver's name. Pledges were vital to covering the church's annual budget. Cash donations were gravy. But the church had been spending heavily with its rapid growth, and was deeply in debt. Some of that cash was needed to cover costs.

"Shouldn't the funds show up as a deposit to the other account?" the shorter man asked.

"I've kept that account off the books for now, so the board won't bog themselves down over it. Some of them, you know, are not visionary thinkers. They fret about little stuff -- buying a new first aid kit or replacing a fire extinguisher – because it's what they can relate to. We've got a couple of bean counters on the board who worry excessively about making ends meet and maybe don't see the same upside you and I do. Believe me, in one good Sunday we can blow the lid off donations."

The shorter man rested his chin on his hand and thought. "We have some balances due for contractors that we need to pay. Some of these are pretty big. We need an explanation for the board if they ask about the lean donations."

"As far as the contractors go, that's no problem at all. I'll take care of them," the taller man said. "Most will write off those balances as donations to the church. Our support is so important to them; they'd be crazy not to take the offer."

"I'm amazed at what you can do with the power of your personality and persuasion," the shorter man said, shaking his head.

"A smile opens doors in almost any discussion. As for the board, I need you to reassure them that we're working on something special that will glorify God. If you'll back me on this, they won't ask many questions."

"I hope not."

"Don't sell yourself short. The DeGroot name carries a great deal of influence in this community. You have a lot of friends for your steadfast support of the Navy and economic development. That goes for your parents, too, who are remembered as leaders in county and city government. I'll be there to pitch in if you need my backing, but I'll bet it doesn't even come to that."

Then he added, "While I'm thinking of it, I have a little something for you as a token of my appreciation for the leadership you are showing on our board, and your unfailing support, friendship and loyalty toward me personally."

He reached into the breast pocket of his sport jacket and

retrieved a fat envelope, which he handed to the shorter man. "Fifty thousand dollars," he said. "Tax-free, all cash."

"I couldn't possibly . . ."

"You could and I insist that you do, because you're a pillar of this ministry and I rely on you more than I can ever adequately express. Take it with the Lord's blessing, and mine. God wants you to prosper."

"But what about Grace King? I'm worried about what she could do to us if you don't have her under control," the shorter man said. "Isn't she on the verge of going public with her accusations? If we can't stop her somehow this whole thing will blow up in our faces."

"It's all cleared up now."

"You talked her out of it?"

"The exact details aren't important -- it was all a misunderstanding. The matter was between her and me, and the Lord. I prayed on it and the Lord delivered a solution. You may hear things that are upsetting, but just know that His will has been done. That's a good way to leave it for now, I think. No need for you to worry about it."

Visitors

Kat looked out across the rolling, plowed earth of Ebey's Prairie. The light was soft and the shadows were long. The sun was just cresting the Cascade Mountains as she and Shane neared Coupeville's main highway intersection on their way to the sheriff's department. The sky was clear and Shane wanted to make sure Kat got a good look at the stunning view of Mount Baker and Penn Cove.

"This early-morning light takes your breath away," Kat said, looking west across the fields. Shane told her the original settlers had chosen their land well, homesteading here and establishing farms still owned, in some cases, by their descendants.

"Some people find it hard to handle the winters here," Shane said. "The overcast and short hours of daylight make them sad, so they head for their second homes in Arizona. But I find I'm so busy all the time, I don't give it a thought. I like living in a place that has all four seasons."

He changed the subject. "We've got a break in the search for George and Nadya. The Lexus is parked across the road from the Keystone Ferry landing, which means they probably walked aboard as foot passengers to Port Townsend. We're checking lodgings within walking distance of the Port Townsend landing now." With luck, you and I will run over there today and drop in on them.

At the office, Shane ordered DNA and fingerprinting of all the principal suspects, and instructed his associates to dust the bedroom, shop and truck for fingerprints, as well as containers of cleaning products such as bleach, and tools such as the hammer in George's shop. "If we find Kapinski's fingerprints on anything inside the house, it will be damning for him," he said. "Same with the boyfriend, David, if his DNA or fingerprints turn up in the wrong places. Or Cordell Wurm."

By ten a.m., the office had identified the luxury B&B where George and Nadya were registered in Port Townsend. "Want to take a ferry ride?" Shane asked Kat.

"Sure."

As they drove to Keystone, Shane called Elizabeth and filled her in on what they were doing. "I don't know what time we'll get back, but there is only one boat on the run in the winter. The sailings are widely spaced, so we might be an hour or two late tonight."

"I'll see you when you get here," Elizabeth said. "Good luck today."

The next boat wasn't scheduled to leave until 11:45 a.m., so after Shane and Kat parked, they walked over to the café for an early lunch. As they walked, Kat looked up as a high-pitched chatter passed overhead.

"What is that?" she asked.

"A male Belted Kingfisher."

"You know your birds," Kat said.

The bird landed on the floodgate next to the café. "They often hang out right here to fish in Crockett Lake. They hover and then drop straight down into the water and come up with a fish."

"Cool."

"Yes, it is. Crockett Lake and Keystone Spit are right next to each other and they're a major destination for birders. In addition to all the year-round 'regulars,' and lots of raptors, many flocks of migrating birds stop here."

"I'll bet Elizabeth likes it," Kat said.

Shane smiled. "She certainly does."

The trip across to Port Townsend was smooth and quiet. Kat spent part of it out on the deck, soaking up the sights and smells of the sea. The sun felt good. As they neared Port Townsend she was excited to see several expressive, whiskered faces looking up at her from the water alongside the boat. Shane said the curious mammals were harbor seals.

In Port Townsend, they lost no time heading uptown to the Widow's Walk Inn. Shane introduced himself and Kat to the manager, who paged the room. George and Nadya apparently were out, which was their usual routine, he said. Shane said they'd wait in the parlor, where they could keep an eye on the front door.

The lovebirds appeared about 3 p.m., walking arm in arm. Shane could tell that George was surprised to see him.

"Mr. King, could we have a word somewhere private, perhaps your room?" Shane asked.

"Of course," George replied. "This is quite a surprise."

"I imagine it is," Shane allowed.

The four of them climbed the wide, curving stairs to the second floor. As they walked, Nadya opened her mouth several times as if on the verge of speaking, but no words came out.

Shane filled the silence. "I must say we were surprised to find you not at your home in Greenbank. We've positively identified your wife through dental records and need you to take responsibility for her remains and funeral arrangements. We also served a search warrant on you the other day and entered your house to look for evidence in connection with the disappearance of your wife. We've impounded two computers."

"You must be kidding," George remarked as he unlocked the door to the room. "I can't work without my computer. Do you seriously consider me a suspect?"

Shane shrugged.

In the room, Nadya put down her shopping bags. She and Kat seated themselves on the edge of the bed to watch. George and Shane sat in two wing chairs, facing each other.

"Here's the problem," Shane began. "Your wife, Grace, was murdered in your bed at 6:02 a.m., December 24th, and her body was left in that bed until 4:42 p.m. There is blood spatter all over the floor and wall of your bedroom. It's been cleaned up, but we can see it clearly with forensic tests."

"Oh my god," Nadya blurted. "Where we slept."

"There's a big blood spot in your shop that has not been cleaned up at all, and there's still more blood in the back of your truck," he said, nodding toward Kat. "Your wife disappeared Christmas Eve, the day Nadya here arrived for a romantic visit. This all looks pretty damning," Shane said, "and I'd like to know how you explain it."

"Oh god," George said, raising both hands to his head. "Oh god. I wish there were some way to find her boyfriend but I don't even have a name."

"We found him," Shane said. "We talked to him and we're still checking him out."

"Really?" George asked. "How?"

"We got lucky."

Shane continued, "Did you know that your neighbor, Zeke Kapinski, has been spying on you and Grace?"

"What?" George asked. "That isn't possible."

"We talked to him and he admitted it. He gave us a lot of information about comings and goings at the house. We're still nailing down the timeline."

"Well then he must be the one who did it," George said. "Someone got into the house and murdered Grace while I was away. If Kapinski has been watching us, it all adds up. That's the only explanation that makes sense."

"Tell me again exactly when you were away from your home."

"The night of December 23 and most of December 24. It's complicated," George said, rubbing his face with both hands and looking at the floor.

Nadya stared at him. "Where were you the night of December 23?" she asked him.

"I needed to talk with someone. Everything was piling up on me. I was with a friend. That's all."

"Overnight?" She asked.

Nadya shook her head, looked at Shane, and shrugged.

"I'm going to need the name of this person," Shane said, "to verify your alibi."

"Have you talked to Pastor Tom?" George asked.

"Who?"

"He's that sleaze ball preacher at the Prosperity Bible Church. Grace fell in with that crowd a while back."

"The guy who drives a Rolls Royce?"

"That's him. You should talk to him. Real snake. Grace fell for his slick act – hook, line and sinker. I know he came to the house several times, and Grace did a lot of so-called counseling with him at the church. I wouldn't be surprised if he's involved in what happened. Between the boyfriend and the preacher, I think she got herself into a real jam."

"So that's one more for us to check on," Shane said, turning toward Kat. She scribbled the information into a notepad.

"Mr. King, can you think of anyone who might have a reason to harm your wife?" Shane asked. George screwed up his face as if to respond, but apparently thought better of it and said nothing. Shane felt he was holding back.

"I need to ask you again, where were you the night of December 23?" Shane reminded him.

"Could I have a word with you privately out in the hall?" George asked. George stepped into the hall and Shane followed, pulling the door shut behind them.

"Here's what I don't understand," Shane said. "If you weren't the killer, how would he have known he could leave the body lying in the house all day on Christmas Eve, and you wouldn't be coming home to discover it?"

"Grace must have told him. I told her I would be gone most of the 23rd and 24th, but that by evening on Christmas Eve she needed to be somewhere else."

When they returned to the room, Shane said, "I'm not going to arrest you today, but I'd like you to go back home so we can talk some more in the coming days."

Ordinarily the house would be considered a crime scene, Shane said. But the department had finished its investigation and left a copy of the search warrant at the scene, and removed what they wanted to study.

"Ok," George said. "I want to cooperate. I know I've made a mess of things, but someone is framing me for something I didn't do."

"We'll be in touch," Shane said.

Back on the ferry, Shane could tell Kat's mind was churning with the new developments. "Do you believe him?" she asked.

"I don't know. He has a problem with the truth."

"What was Grace going to blow the lid off of?" Shane asked. "Did it get her killed?"

"Maybe," Kat continued. "If Grace was trying to end something with her boyfriend, David, and getting involved in a new romantic liaison with Pastor Tom, she might have been pretty confused."

"We don't know there was anything romantic between them."

"No, but it sounds like it. And if she blew the lid off their relationship – went public with his adultery – maybe it could take down the church."

"Would adultery be enough to bring him down? I'm just asking," Shane said, before adding, "There's something else about George."

"I wondered," Kat said. "What was so sensitive he couldn't talk about it in front of Nadya and me?"

"George had a romantic affair a couple of months ago with Dr. Joyce Haycourt, a local ear-nose-and-throat specialist who owns a clinic on the island. He went to talk with her again just a few days ago, because she refused to accept it was over. He didn't want her showing up and making a scene while Nadya was here and ruining his chances with her. That's where he was on December 23, trying to lay things to rest once and for all with her. He didn't want to bring her up in front of Nadya."

"What a mess."

"It's even messier than that, because he says Joyce is mentally unstable, drinking and using drugs. He thinks the clinic is in debt and teetering on failure because Joyce is running up huge lawyer's fees. She's desperate for him to leave Grace, and thinks Grace is all that stands between the two of them. He doesn't know what she's capable of, but says she certainly had a motive to do Grace harm. He just doesn't know whether she would act on it."

"The timing is suspicious," Kat said. "George talks to her on December 23, and the next day Grace is dead."

Pastor Tom

Shane and Kat sat in facing chairs on the ferry, deep in thought as they made the quiet crossing back to Whidbey Island. Kat caught herself smiling several times and wondered if it was obvious to Shane her mind was somewhere else. Finally, Kat looked up and asked Shane to fill her in on Pastor Tom.

With the caveat that he was no expert on evangelists, Shane said the pastor and his wife, Charity, showed up on the island several years earlier and started holding revival meetings in public parks and community halls. They moved here from New Zealand, where they'd gotten into some trouble with local authorities, the details of which had never been clear to Shane. They had a small rock band that performed up-tempo Christian music to entertain the crowd. He'd heard they put on a good show.

Pastor Tom preached a blend of flag-waving patriotism and God's wish for his flock to prosper beyond their wildest dreams if they were generous in their giving, Shane said. On the island, with its large military community in Oak Harbor, patriotism and religion were a potent mix, and Tom was a charismatic speaker.

Skillfully woven into his pitch was the notion that providing for the pastor and his wife was the congregation's job one. So the church directors paid him a large salary, including travel and living expenses, and gave him lavish gifts. The pastor's leased Rolls Royce was one of the perks.

"Sounds like the Bhagwan Shree Rajneesh all over again," Kat said, bringing up the Indian guru who founded a spiritual commune in the 1980s near Antelope, in Eastern Oregon. "Cults fascinate me and I've done a lot of reading about them. Rajneesh's followers gave him a large fleet of luxury cars, mostly Rolls Royces, before everything came crashing down," she said. "His subordinates got caught breaking numerous laws, including attempted mass poisoning with salmonella by tampering with a salad bar in The Dalles. Their plan was to get several members of the commune elected as county commissioners by suppressing the turnout of local residents. The commune bused in homeless people from all over the country to live in Rajneeshpuram, asking only that they become registered to vote in the county and help elect the commune's slate of candidates.

"Why do so many people suspend belief and put their trust in these corrupt spiritual guides and evangelists?" Kat asked.

"I think about that a lot," Shane replied. "I'm afraid it's all part of the dumbing-down of America, the same thing we see in politics, where people believe what they *want* to believe, without applying critical thinking. We're being taught that truth and integrity don't matter any more – just spreading your agenda. A charlatan can get away with anything if he tells people what they want to hear."

He continued, "By invoking God's name, there isn't much these preachers can't justify or rationalize. Maybe their followers actually take a perverse comfort from their pastors' human shortcomings, since it essentially lowers the bar for them. It demonstrates Satan can tempt even the most exalted of role models, so if they fall short in some way, too, it's not that serious. The roster of disgraced televangelists and mega-church pastors is just endless – Ted Haggard, Jim Bakker, Jimmy Swaggart, Bill Gothard, and on and on.

"All these spiritual guides seem to do pretty well with the same general formula for exploiting people's gullibility," Shane continued. He went on to say that Pastor Tom built a large church outside Coupeville that can seat 4,000 at a time, and it often fills up on Sundays. In the summertime he still moves services outside sometimes to accommodate even larger crowds and let the congregation enjoy the sunshine.

"So where do Tom and Charity live?" Kat asked. "Can we go there now?"

"Yes to your second question. I've never been there but I know where it is. As for the first, they live in a gated compound on West Beach Road, an area of the best view homes on a high bluff looking out to sea and the shipping lanes."

It was 5:30, well past winter sunset and darkness, when Shane and Kat got back to their car at Keystone. "We can get to West Beach in half an hour," Shane said. "The timing is a little awkward with the dinner hour, but let's see if they let us in. Give Elizabeth a call so she knows how our time is running."

They drove past Coupeville and continued north for about five minutes, then turned left on Libbey Road and right on West Beach Road, which followed the shoreline north. A few minutes later they pulled up to the wrought-iron gate and Shane pressed the intercom.

"Yes?" said a raspy voice on the intercom.

"Detective Shane Lindstrom and Kat Brown. We'd like a few minutes of the pastor's time in connection with an active police investigation."

"Do you have an appointment?"

"No."

"Just a moment."

The gate buzzed and swung open. Shane and Kat drove up the circular driveway to the front door and parked behind the pastor's black Rolls Royce Phantom and a white, limited edition Jaguar. Shane was curious about the Jag and took a closer look.

Kat was learning his trick of looking for webcams. Right away she spotted three of them, one of which was sweeping back and forth across the front entryway in a wide arc. There was nowhere out front to escape the sweep of that camera, except maybe flat against the building."

Even at night, or maybe because it was night, the large, brick house and its outbuildings were stunning. Kat would never forget her first impression of this place. Light poured from every window and spilled onto the manicured lawn.

A large US flag waved in the onshore breeze, illuminated by floodlights, and the hardware in its halyard clanged against the pole. The pastor and Charity answered the door with beaming smiles, the very picture of health, prosperity and plenty of sex, Kat thought.

"Welcome, detective. This is an unexpected surprise," Pastor Tom said, extending his hand. "Please come in."

Kat noticed the pastor's choice of words. She wondered if he had started out to say "unexpected pleasure" but just couldn't bring himself to do it.

"This is Miss Brown," Shane said, "my associate," and they both shook hands with her. The pastor held onto Kat's hand with both of his, examining it a little longer than she was comfortable with.

"How may we help you?"

"We wondered how well you knew Grace King, a member of your congregation," Shane began.

"Sister Grace? We were quite close. Lovely woman with a real hunger to know the Lord," the pastor replied. "I was doing some counseling with her."

"What can you tell me about the topics of that counseling?"

"Well, all counseling is confidential, but I can tell you broadly it had to do with marriage and the Lord's plans for her life, our expectations around giving, and how she could best serve the Lord – that kind of thing."

"Grace won't have much need for confidentiality now," Shane pointed out.

Kat caught the pastor's eyes scanning up and down her body while he answered Shane's question. It made her uneasy.

"Did she have any problems or worries that were particularly weighing on her?"

"You understand I have to be careful not to betray a confidence," the pastor said. "You speak of her in the past tense. Is there some reason for that?"

"Yes, we are trying to determine who murdered her."

"Grace? Oh no."

Charity joined in. "Murder? Not Grace. Are you sure?"

Shane nodded.

"When did this happen?" Charity asked.

"At 6:02 a.m., Christmas Eve," Shane said.

Shane's answer had the desired effect. Pastor Tom winced, no doubt shocked at Shane's precision and how much more he might know that he wasn't saying.

"I understand Grace had a boyfriend and we're wondering if you knew anything about the state of their relationship."

"This is the first I've heard of it."

"Have you seen Grace recently?" Shane asked.

"No, not that I recall. I think it was sometime before Christmas, at the church."

"Do you know anyone who might wish her harm?" Shane asked.

"Again, I feel an obligation to choose my words carefully. I'll just say what you probably already know, that her relationship with her husband was troubled. That was part of the reason she sought comfort in the church."

"That's what we've heard."

Shane reached into his pocket and took out a business card. "I know it's dinnertime and we don't want to delay yours any more tonight. If you think of anything that might help us, please give me a call."

"Certainly, detective and Miss Brown. The Lord bless you both for this important work you're doing."

Frauds

"What a pair of frauds!" Kat exploded when they got back into the car and closed the doors behind them. "Like two grinning bobble head dolls. I don't believe one word that came out of his mouth. And those fake smiles!"

"So other than that, what did you think of the good pastor?" Shane asked, and they both laughed. "Quite the man of God."

"He's creepy," Kat observed. "Did you see him leering at me? I wouldn't want to be alone with him."

She added, "I love the license plates on their cars: I M LORD on his and OBEY HIM on hers. At least I assume the Jaguar was her car."

"I think so."

Kat had a hard time stopping the convulsions of laughter. "I think I'm rummy from the long day," she gasped. She pulled herself together and continued, "Did you notice how slyly he tried to throw suspicion toward George King, 'while choosing his words carefully' as he put it."

"I sure did. Now, sit back and relax. We'll be home in no time," Shane said. "I cut the interview short because it was obvious we were just wasting our time. The paper had an article a few weeks ago about several members of his congregation who got disgruntled and left. Maybe we can catch up with a couple of them and get a different take on things."

*

On his computer screen, Pastor Tom watched the webcam as they got into their car and drove away. Charity looked over his shoulder.

"What do you think?" she asked.

"Lightweights," he said. "They've got nothing. They were just going through the motions of constructing a picture of Grace's life. We won't hear any more from them."

When Kat and Shane got home, Shane went digging in the closet for the newspaper he remembered and reread the interview with the church dissidents. Then he called a couple of the former church members who had spoken to the newspaper reporter and asked if they would meet with him at nine o'clock the next morning, at the sheriff's department. They both agreed eagerly.

Shane and Kat filled in Elizabeth on their fascinating meetings with George and Nadya in Port Townsend, and Pastor Tom and Charity at their West Beach home.

Soon, she was laughing along with them.

"This case just keeps expanding outward and getting more complicated," Shane said. "I've never seen anything like it."

"Think about poor me," Kat said. "I feel like I'm cramming four years of sociology and police studies into two weeks."

"You'll be able to teach the course by the time you leave here," Shane said. "And by the way, you're the most fun of any partner I've ever had."

Kat smiled.

*

Dr. Joyce Haycourt sat slumped at her desk, with her head in her hands and a half-empty bottle of vodka in front of her. She had been sleeping poorly for days, had stopped taking her anti-depressants and had been having suicidal thoughts in the two weeks leading up to Christmas. She knew all about the warnings not to mix alcohol and drugs.

It was bad enough that the holidays were a season of forced joy and family togetherness, but this December had been especially cruel with the divorce and the strain on her finances. At best it was always a lean month, made worse by vacations of patients and staff, and appointment cancellations. Christmas and New Year's Eve cut into the clinic's income, but this year she would have to put off some suppliers to meet payroll.

It was nearly seven p.m. and she'd been drinking on an empty stomach for two hours. She wanted to talk to George and had left several messages on his cell phone, but he was not answering and not returning her calls.

She put the vodka in her briefcase, locked her desk, removed her winter coat from the hook behind the door, and turned out the light. She let herself out the employee entrance in back that opened to the parking lot, and reset the security system behind her. Her cherry red Miata was the only car in the lot. The parking lot still had some ice on it and she wasn't that steady. She slid and lost her balance momentarily on the pavement, which had never fully thawed from the Christmas Eve snowstorm.

She started the engine, turned the defroster on full, and retrieved the bottle from her briefcase. She placed the bottle on the passenger seat and started to drive. On the outskirts of Oak Harbor she ran a red light, dodging several other cars as she did it. A city police car pulled into the lane behind her, sped up to close the gap, and turned on its flashers. Haycourt sped up a little, too, rolling through several more intersections without slowing or stopping for lights and cross traffic.

At a reasonably conservative forty-five miles per hour she passed the turnoff to the Naval Air Station, still leading the city police car, and accelerated as she left the congested urban area behind.

*

Kat was already seated at the conference table, doing something on her iPhone, when Shane showed the middle-age couple into the room. When they entered, she put it down and shook hands with each, and everyone sat down. The man placed a manila envelope on the table in front of him.

"Thank you for calling us in," the man said.

Shane asked the couple to explain briefly about their backgrounds. The man, about six feet tall, and stocky, was a retired Navy supply clerk whose home business now was to build cedar lawn furniture in his shop. He sold the furniture at local festivals and street fairs. He also volunteered as a dog-walker one day a week at the animal shelter. The woman ran an accounting business, helping mostly elderly clients with their tax returns. She volunteered at the community food bank.

"It's nice someone takes us seriously enough to be willing to meet with us," the man said. "After the article in the paper, we thought there might be more fallout and perhaps an investigation, but the whole thing just blew over. The church takes out a big, full-page ad in the paper every week, you know."

"Yeah, they place ads," the woman said, "but I don't know if they actually pay for them."

"What can you tell us about the Prosperity Bible Church? What is going on there?" Shane asked.

"It's a shell game with money," the woman said. "Pastor Tom moves money around so freely that no one knows where it goes. Certainly not the board. None of the authorities or political leaders in the county want to question what he does. He contributes generously to their campaigns."

"How did you end up challenging what was happening financially at the church?" Shane asked, looking at the woman.

"Well first of all, I'm a member – or I was – and so are many of my clients. As I prepared their tax returns, many were giving staggering amounts to the church. These are people who have very little to spare in the first place."

"Did you know Grace King?" Shane asked.

"Yes, I did. Quite a nice person, but I think she got in over her head. She was one of Pastor Tom's girlfriends."

"You're saying Pastor Tom was playing around behind his wife's back?"

"Not behind it but with Charity's full knowledge and participation. She does the same thing."

Shane turned to the man. "You brought an envelope. Do you have something to show us?"

The man nodded, opened the flap and pulled a sheet of paper from it. He put the sheet in front of Shane and turned it so he could read it, and then pointed.

"This is the treasurer's record of donations over the last eight weeks. I have a friend on the board who gave this to me on a strict promise that I not mention his name."

Shane glanced at the numbers. "There's a big drop here in December."

"Yes, and the only explanation is that the pastor isn't reporting everything he's taking in. The easiest place to under-report is in cash donations to the collection plate."

"And the board just goes along with this?" Shane asked, rolling his eyes.

"Yes, for some reason that I can only assume is bribery."

"So backing up a bit, what caused you to break with the pastor?" Shane asked him.

"It was the way he manipulated the young Navy personnel," he said. "Many of them are from the South and have grown up in the evangelical tradition. He is very skillful at exploiting that, and their patriotism. He knows how to blur the line between God and country."

"Are you evangelical as well?" Shane asked.

"No, I'm Christian reformed. Grew up right here in Oak Harbor."

"Also," the man added, "the sheer hypocrisy was hard to take. The pastor doesn't talk about it publicly, but he and Charity have an open marriage. The Bible, the way Pastor Tom interprets it, says God wants us to be happy. That means it's okay to have sex with anyone and everyone we want. The pastor was grooming Grace to be part of their special circle."

"That sounds like Bhagwan Rajneesh again," Kat piped up. "Sorry. I read a book."

"Do you know if Grace was having second thoughts about what she'd gotten into with the church and Pastor Tom?

"I'm sure she was," the woman said. "The pastor is very charming. He can make you believe up is down. That's why the church has grown so fast. On the one hand Grace was drawn to his magnetic personality and flattered that he found her attractive. On the other hand she was badly confused and conflicted after she got to know him. She had also started talking to us, providing details we hadn't heard before. She was debating whether to go public with the scandal in the church."

"What is the scandal?" Shane asked. "Financial? Sexual?"

"Both, and probably more. The pastor is raking off thousands of dollars in church donations on top of his excessive salary."

"Isn't there a board that exercises some oversight?"

"Are you kidding?" the woman asked. "They're all sycophants

and are well compensated to play along. They will rubber-stamp anything he wants. We've wondered for a long time where the money is going. If he's siphoning it off, no one on the board will stand up and challenge him."

"Can you give me a list of the board members?"

"Of course," she said. Shane handed her a legal pad and she began writing names. First on the list was Charlie DeGroot. The name rang a bell – Dutch and Dorothy DeGroot's son. The DeGroots were crooked real estate developers and local politicians. Shane had exposed their activities several years earlier. Dutch was behind bars. Dorothy committed suicide.

"I see you've written Charlie DeGroot," Shane said. "Is he pretty involved in the church's business?"

"That would be putting it mildly," the man acknowledged. "Charlie is president of the board and also the pastor's right-hand man."

"So he might be aware of the embezzling?"

"If not actively involved."

Shane was taken aback to run into the DeGroot name again. Several years ago Shane had arrested Charlie's parents for murder on the Alaska Ferry. The man whose murder they orchestrated was the brother of the woman who became Shane's wife, Elizabeth.

The man continued, "Pastor Tom was very angry about our little breakaway group. He never stops smiling but lets you know you'll pay a steep price if you turn against him. With his sexual liaisons, he reminds you that everything is consensual, and if you betray him he'll drag your name and reputation through the mud. It's not easy to go up against him. If you push too hard he'll call you Satan in the flesh, and his followers will tend to believe, unquestioningly, whatever he says."

Shane remarked, "Grace told a friend she was thinking about blowing the lid off something, but didn't say what. It sounds like it may have been this."

"I think so," the woman said.

"And if it turns out Pastor Tom had anything to do with her death, that will really blow the lid off," Shane said.

*

Shane and Kat had just come out of their meeting when they got the news of the highway fatality overnight. Shane was used to hearing of head-on collisions on the winding, two-lane corridor of Highway 20 that connects Skagit and Island counties across the picturesque Deception Pass Bridge. Young drivers took the curves too fast, and elderly drivers sometimes misjudged another car's speed. This was different.

A prominent local doctor had lost control and crashed her sports car near the bridge while fleeing from Oak Harbor city police and county sheriff's deputies. Alcohol and drugs were believed to be involved, and may have been the reason she fled an otherwise routine traffic stop.

Oak Harbor police had attempted to stop her, initially opting for a low-speed chase in light of the icy conditions and the danger to pedestrians and other drivers. They had hoped the driver would come to her senses and pull over. When she didn't, they were later joined by sheriff's deputies as the doctor's car approached the bridge, about to cross into Skagit County at excessively high speed. The sheriff's deputies placed a roadblock across the highway at the bridge. Dr. Haycourt turned away from the roadblock, lost control and wrapped her car around a four-hundred-year-old fir tree. She was killed outright. The tree sustained almost no damage.

It struck Shane as an entirely unnecessary tragedy, a well-regarded doctor caught in personal and financial circumstances beyond her ability to cope. Problems that might have seemed hopeless to her today would likely look entirely different in a few months or a year from now, but she would never get the chance to find out.

Shane and Kat sat and pondered what they'd just heard. Kat twirled a lock of her hair with her finger as she thought, and was the first to speak.

"We won't get to question Dr. Haycourt," Kat said, "but Pastor Tom certainly has a motive to harm Grace. His entire scam could come crashing down in disgrace, ending a very lucrative lifestyle. We need to know if he has an alibi for the time of the murder. It would be nice to catch him in a lie about that. We could use a witness, but I doubt Charity will contradict his version of events."

"I think we should ask them, just to get them on the record,"

Shane replied. "I'll have Donovan bring them in and follow up. If we split them up, they may give different accounts."

"That's a good idea."

"And regarding a witness, we may have one. Remember how Zeke Kapinski clammed up when I asked if he knew where Grace King was? I think he saw more than he wanted to say. If Pastor Tom went to the house, Kapinski may have seen him. We should talk with Kapinski again. If he understands that we're not trying to pin something on him, he may be more willing to share what he knows with us."

Shane had long believed that people who lie eventually trip over their own untruths. The web of deceit is too hard to remember and defend against contradictory evidence. Little by little, Shane and Kat were peeling back the lies told by their suspects and finding the truth – King, Kapinski and Pastor Tom. Kapinski might be constructing an elaborate deception to hide what he'd done and throw suspicion on others, but he was also adding to their picture of Grace and George's lives.

At Kapinski's house, Shane's knock on the door brought movement of a curtain. "I already told you what I know," Kapinski shouted through the door.

"We have some developments regarding a new suspect and need your help again," Shane yelled back.

The door opened. "Let's do our talking out here," Kapinski said.

"I'll get right to the point. On December 23rd or 24th, did you notice any strange vehicles at the house while Grace was home alone?"

"Cars come and go a lot. I might have."

"Can you describe what you saw?"

"Why don't you come in? It's too cold to stand out here." Kapinski pointed to the couch, and Shane and Kat sat down.

Kapinski reached over to a side table where he had an open pack of Camels. He shook one from the pack, stuck it between his lips and struck a paper match to light it. He shook the match out, and dropped it into an ashtray. Then he took a couple of puffs, exhaled and looked at Shane.

"One of those English luxury cars," he said.

"When was that?"

"It was there on the 23rd and again when I got back from picking up a load of logs on the peninsula on the 24th. It left soon after I got home."

"Did it look anything like this?" Shane asked, showing Kapinski a photocopy of a late-model Rolls Royce in black."

"Yeah."

"Can you remember the license plate?"

"Yeah, I can. It was odd – I M LORD."

"Why didn't you bring this up when we talked with you before?"

"Because I don't need any more trouble. You don't mess with people who drive those cars. Those people have power, and friends in high places."

*

"That was crucial," Shane said when they got back into their car. "Kapinski just put Pastor Tom at the scene with a positive I.D. of his vehicle. That's the break we've been looking for. That is just huge."

Praise the Lord

Kat looked around her and surveyed the crowd at the Prosperity Bible Church. All 4,000 seats were filled. One of the ushers announced on the public address system that hundreds more worshipers were packed into the entryway and watching on TV monitors. Kat had arrived an hour early and chosen a seat near the front of the room.

The crowd swayed to the beat of a Christian rock band with an especially good drummer. Red, yellow, blue and green spotlights swept back and forth across the stage and reflected off a rotating disco ball. The room shook. Kat could feel the energy in her bones. She had goose bumps on her arms. This was not a church but a phenomenon!

The drummer finished with a flourish. The music suddenly stopped and Pastor Tom and Charity ran onto the stage from behind a curtain, and stepped up to the podium. The crowd whistled and clapped. The pastor and his wife smiled broadly and raised their arms to signal the crowd to be silent.

"Please. Please," Pastor Tom spoke. "Please." He and Charity were flawlessly tailored, he in a dark blue suit with a red tie and styled black hair, and she in a white dress, her blonde tresses cascading down her back. "Thank you," the pastor said. "Thank you. Please . . . please."

"Good morning, Christians!" Tom began. "Today will be the *best* day of your life."

"Amen and alellujah," Charity spoke into her headset, clapping her hands and holding both arms over her head and bowing. "Praise the Lord!"

"Praise the Lord," echoed more than 4,000 voices.

"I know why you're happy," he said, borrowing a line from the comedian, Bill Maher. "It's because God loves you."

"Now, please be seated," Tom instructed the crowd. He held a Bible in his right hand and a plastic water bottle in his left. As he waited for the group to settle down he paced back and forth, letting the suspense build. He took a sip of water and put the bottle down on a tall stool. He looked right at the crowd as if to speak, right at Kat, but then reconsidered. Anticipation built in the quiet hall as he looked down at the floor, then up at the rafters, deep in concentration or prayer. Kat wasn't sure which. What was going through that mind?

Kat looked around at the congregation. There were many white faces but also many black – young Navy personnel and their spouses, she assumed, from the large base north of Oak Harbor.

"Brothers and sisters in Christ, why am I here?" Pastor Tom began. "And why are *you* here? We are here to worship the Lord. And the Lord wants us to prosper. It's as simple as that. He wants good health and wealth for us, good families, good marriages, even good sex!"

The congregation laughed nervously. A few men pumped their fists in the air.

"But the blessings he has in store for us are not free," the pastor said, his smile suddenly replaced by an earnestly serious expression. His voice dropped to almost a whisper, forcing the four thousand worshipers to lean forward and listen closely. "We prosper in proportion to the love and devotion, and yes, gifts, we lay at the master's feet. Giving is so important.

"I see a sister in the crowd today, someone new, a doubter that the Lord has led to our fold, and I pray she will find salvation today. He looked right at Kat. I look around this hall and see others who are sick, burdened with the weight of chronic illness. Some are awaiting a diagnosis that will rock them to the core. How do we deal with such shocking truth? Well I have good news. We trust in the Lord. The Lord wants us to be well!"

"Praise the Lord," Charity said.

"Praise the Lord," the crowd echoed.

Pastor Tom wasted no time getting personal, picking out faces in the crowd, and making the all-important pitch for donations, Kat thought.

"I want to say a special welcome to our Navy friends. We love the Navy, the sound of freedom and those Growlers you fly!" he declared. The crowd broke into applause. Kat knew the reference to Growlers was to the current generation of Navy aircraft with the ear-splitting shriek, that have been so controversial on Whidbey Island, and all across Puget Sound and the Olympic Peninsula. The Navy felt besieged by opponents. The town of Oak Harbor was worried about losing its economic engine. Pastor Tom was giving this crowd just what they wanted to hear. God was on their side.

"The ushers will pass the collection plates after awhile. When they do, I hope you will give from the heart until it hurts, because whatever you give will be repaid to you tenfold. Do your part and the Lord will do his."

He added, "God wants to put material wealth into your hands. I didn't come here to get anything from you. I'm already LOADED!"

Wow! She thought. She had never heard a preacher say that!

An usher tapped Kat on the shoulder. "Pastor Tom wants to thank you for attending today. He remembers meeting you the other day and would love to talk with you more after the service if you'd care to join him."

Kat was astounded at the personal invitation and at Pastor Tom's outright brazenness. She would have a lot to report to Shane and Elizabeth when she got home today.

*

Nadya stood in the living room of George's house with her hands on her hips, looking at him. "Look at my eyes," she demanded. "I'm asking you straight, did you murder wife?" They had just gotten back from Port Townsend and were unpacking.

"No," George said, rubbing his face as she'd seen him do before when he was stressed. "Absolutely not."

"There is so much evidence. How do you explain your garage, your truck?"

"Someone is framing me. I don't know why."

Much as Nadya loved the United States, the country baffled her. Almost every day, a mass shooter somewhere mowed down innocent strangers for no good reason. Violence was everywhere, and she wondered if George was just one more sick person who murdered because it was so easy to do in this country.

"Your wife was murdered in this house. In that bed," Nadya said, shaking her finger in the direction of the bedroom. "I cannot spend one more minute in that bed."

"We'll move into the guest room."

"Tell me about you and your wife. The truth." Nadya demanded.

George asked her to sit down in an easy chair in the living room. He chose a chair nearby and sat silent for a moment, then began. He said he and Grace were married in 1991.

"End of Soviet Union," Nadya remarked.

"What?"

"That's the year Soviet Union dissolved and became Russian Federation."

"Oh," George said. "How was that for you?"

"Good. Exciting. Gorbachev good man – progressive. At first I thought we would become prosperous like USA. But it didn't last. Space program kaput. National pride gone. Yeltsin alcoholic. Putin come along – KGB man – with criminal friends, rich oligarchs, and it all went back to the corrupt old ways."

George waited till she finished, and then went back to his story. The marriage got off to a good start, he said, because he and Grace were both professionals, both loved nature and the outdoors, and both wanted to live on the island.

"We found this house and thought it was everything we'd dreamed."

But as happens sometimes, George said he and Grace grew in opposite directions. They both poured themselves into their careers, which kept them traveling separately for long periods of time. Finding himself in strange cities for weeks at a time, George admitted he drifted into unfaithfulness, and he was pretty sure Grace did, too.

"What was it, do you think, that caused you to want to be unfaithful?"

George thought for a moment. "I basically had no one to come home to. I think I've always been insecure about women. With my marriage falling apart, I looked for women to reassure me I'm still desirable."

"What about Grace? What was she looking for in other men?"

"The same thing, probably. I imagine she was lonely."

She nodded. "Who do you think had a motive to kill her and frame you?"

"I've asked myself that over and over. Maybe Kapinski, the voyeur. Maybe the boyfriend. Maybe even the preacher."

"Why would preacher have a motive?"

"Maybe Grace learned something that could hurt him. Powerful men like that often have something to hide. He was looking for big donations and Grace had a good, professional career."

*

At the Eagles Inn B&B, Shane and Elizabeth listened intently as Kat reported on her experience at Pastor Tom's service. "There's no way to adequately describe how it *feels* in that hall – the rush of adrenalin. I can see why people come back week after week and bring their friends."

She had wanted to attend one of his services to better understand who Pastor Tom and Charity really were.

"What do you think he fulfills in the lives of his followers?" Elizabeth asked. "It must be something very basic and deep, almost primal."

"Primal is the right word," Kat said. "I was looking around the room. People seemed consumed with the emotion of the experience – not so much the pastor's words but the feeling. There were lots of young people – young parents. Most of them probably are mired in the daily drudgery of raising families and earning a living – just making ends meet."

Elizabeth nodded. "Young people are the future of the church, but they don't have much money. People like Grace King are the potential big givers."

"I'll say one thing, the collection plate that came down my row was overflowing with $20s and even some $50s. I saw one $100 bill. And there were pledge envelopes, too, from the regular members."

"I'm not surprised," Shane said.

"Just getting through the day must be exhausting for many of the people in that hall," Kat said. "I suppose he offers an escape, a chance to feel something – anything – to lift people out of the numbing routine of their daily lives. He gives a stunning performance. Also, it must be exciting to be part of such a large community of followers."

"That makes sense," Elizabeth said. "What he offers is an intense high. But if you're Pastor Tom, you have to keep topping yourself, and that takes money and lots of it."

"I kept looking at his eyes as he spoke," Kat said, "wondering if they were the eyes of a man who would kill to protect what he has."

"And?" Elizabeth asked.

"Behind the smile, there's an emptiness in his eyes. I believe he would. I think he's capable of anything, while assuring himself it's God's will."

Shane was listening. "I'm dying to ask, did you stay afterwards and meet with Pastor Tom?"

"No, I didn't," Kat said. "I'm playing hard to get."

Forensics

Shane sat with a mug of coffee in the parlor of the Eagles Inn. It was not yet dawn and he was the only member of the household awake. He loved sitting by the window in the early mornings, in the darkness, looking out at the lights of Holmes Harbor, savoring his coffee. Each light had a story – a place where someone's story was being written.

Mornings were when Shane did his best thinking. His mind floated from thought to thought, and sometimes no thoughts at all. Mornings were when he lived in the moment, free from the demands of the job. Someone said, "Life is not a race to get to the end." Many people make themselves so busy, they get to the end never having spent a moment alone with their thoughts.

Looking out from the parlor at night, sometimes he would catch the shadow of a coyote slinking across the yard, a raccoon snooping, or an owl swooping down for a rodent on the lawn. Like him, they were creatures of the night. This morning he was melancholy at the memory of a police colleague who had died in the line of duty. It happened in a small-town café in the Adirondacks of New York, gunned down in a mass shooting targeted specifically at police. Fortunately, Shane usually could shake off the sadness. It was a side of his work he tried not to show Elizabeth, and a reminder never to assume an innocent situation was safe.

He studied the email on his laptop. The forensic results showed the bloodstain on the garage floor and the blood in George King's truck both belonged to Grace King. Shane expected that.

But no fingerprints were found. Well, technically, just one. It was on the shank of the steel hammer from George's shop that presumably was used to bludgeon Grace. Most of it had been wiped clean, but the killer had missed one spot on the upper shaft where there was a perfect thumbprint. Shane didn't know whose print it was, but it did not belong to George. The steering wheel, door handles and other surfaces of George's truck all had been wiped. The circumstantial evidence incriminating George continued to be damning, but Shane thought it peculiar that a man would wipe his own tools and truck clean of fingerprints.

The blood on the running board of Kapinski's truck turned out to be his own. Logging with heavy equipment had its share of scrapes and bruises. Strangely enough, Kapinski wasn't hiding anything about his arm; he was telling the truth. Even a stopped clock tells the truth twice a day. There wasn't anything else honorable about the man.

Pastor Tom had told Donovan a lie about his whereabouts on December 23 and 24. He said he had spent both days at home in his study, working on his Christmas message, and that his wife, Charity, could vouch for it. But Kapinski's memory of the English car with the I M LORD personalized plate specifically contradicted that. The pastor did not know Shane had a witness who could place him at the scene.

Shane tried to imagine what might have been on Grace's mind in the days leading up to Christmas. When did she learn George was bringing a Russian girlfriend into their home? Or did he even tell her that at all? Did he just murder her at the last minute to solve a problem?

Grace's marriage was essentially over – Shane was sure she knew this long before Christmas. But initiating an international mail-order romance was new and bold on George's part. If he had not killed Grace, he had certainly told her she needed to get out of the house by Christmas Eve – he had confessed that directly to Shane when they talked in Port Townsend. Did she call his bluff on that – refuse to go, instead planning to confront the Russian with the truth of her husband's infidelity?

Shane wondered if Grace had been torn between the man she'd been seeing for some time, David, and the charismatic pastor of the church she was attending.

Shane needed to know more about Pastor Tom. Behind the fake sincerity and the plastered-on smile, the pastor was hiding something.

Had Grace started a sexual relationship with Pastor Tom, or

maybe a three-way with Charity, that ended in a jealous rage? Had Grace learned things about the church and its pastor that were so upsetting she was going to blow the lid on the whole organization?

Flawed Men

Shane couldn't get Charlie DeGroot, the board president, out of his mind. Was it possible DeGroot was the killer, or that there were two killers? If DeGroot was involved in Pastor Tom's embezzlement scheme, he would have just as much to lose as the pastor if Grace went public with what she knew.

Shane made a note to have Donovan check DeGroot's whereabouts on December 23 and 24.

The church dissidents had given Shane a look into the circumstances that might have cost Grace her life. If the pastor had killed Grace, was he now preparing to flee? If DeGroot was aware of the pastor's conflict with Grace, or if he participated in her murder, did he also have plans to leave Whidbey Island?

Shane considered both of them flight risks. He needed to talk to DeGroot, but relations between them were not very warm, given that Shane had put his father behind bars, and that his mother had committed suicide. This might be a job for Donovan.

*

"Ok, George," Nadya said. "I make decision to believe you. I hope this is not biggest mistake of my life, but I can't go back-and-forth between wondering if you murdered your wife and listening to you absolutely deny it to my face."

"Thank you," George said, pressing his hands together as if in prayer.

She stepped closer until she was directly in front of him, a foot away. "So I will stay here and support you wherever this leads, and hope the police find the real killer."

She added, "You are flawed man, George King, who has trouble telling truth, but for as long as I stay with you, I expect no less. If you lie to me, there will be hell to pay. She focused an intense stare at him and tapped him hard in the chest with a pointed finger.

"Now, let's get to work boxing up Grace's things, because she has no further need of them."

George got some flattened cartons from the garage and reassembled them with strapping tape. Nadya started in the living room, taking down portraits of Grace, and pictures of both Grace and George as a couple, from the days when their relationship was better. She also removed knick-knacks and lace, paintings and other decorations that reflected Grace's taste.

As soon as they filled a box, George labeled it with a marking pen and carried it to the garage, where he made a stack against the wall. The two of them worked their way to the bedroom closet. "I think the best thing to do with her clothes and shoes is give to charity," Nadya said.

"I agree."

When Nadya got to Grace's old roll-top desk, she slowed down. Grace's laptop computer had been hauled away by the sheriff's department but there were still stacks of letters and printouts in file folders and desk drawers. She found herself scanning them with her eyes as she put them into the box, and stopping to read a few. In a file folder in the lowest drawer she came to a letter Grace had written just a few days ago, December 21.

Dear Pastor Tom,

I have searched my heart and prayed to the Lord for guidance. I am confused about what is happening. You say you are leaving very soon for the Bahamas, never to come back, and you want me to come with you and Charity.

You have told me about Prosperity Island, your refuge, and the large home where we will live together for the rest of our lives. And your yacht, Prosperity. I don't understand how this is possible, where the money comes from. It can only come from one place, and in my heart I know it is wrong.

What about all the people who have trusted you? Dedicated their lives to your message of love and prosperity? To the church? What will this do to them?

I cannot be a part of this. Unless you can assure me that I am terribly misguided, I have no choice but to go public with my concerns.

In Christ,
Grace

"What is this?" Nadya asked, handing the letter to George. He read it quickly and silently.

"It is a bombshell," George said, pulling out his cell phone and dialing.

"Shane Lindstrom."

"This is George King," he said. "Nadya and I are boxing up some of Grace's papers. I've got something here that I think you need to see right now."

*

Shane and Kat reached the King home in less than thirty minutes. Nadya answered the door. Shane could see immediately that something was different in the house. The womanly touches were gone – stripped from the walls.

Nadya led them into the den, where George was looking through more of Grace's papers. He handed Shane the letter, and then waited while Shane read it with Kat looking over his shoulder.

"You found this where?"

"Right there. In a folder in the bottom drawer," George said, pointing at the desk. "Actually, Nadya found it and called me in to look at it. This was Grace's roll top and I stayed out of it for the most part."

"We'll need statements from both of you," George said, "and I'd like to bag this as evidence."

"Of course."

"Are you looking through all those papers pretty carefully?" Shane asked.

"I am now. We're boxing it all anyway, so if there's a need to go back and look some more, we'll still have everything."

Shane tape-recorded their statements, then he and Kat headed for the car.

"This changes everything," he told Kat. "It's like Grace is speaking to us from the grave. We've got a clear motive now and plenty of new questions for the pastor."

"The letter is unsigned," Kat said. "How can we be sure George didn't fabricate it to throw us off?"

"It's always possible, but he'd be foolish to do that. We will soon know if it's real or not, once we confront Pastor Tom and see his reaction."

"It sounds like the pastor is an imminent flight risk, the way Grace talks in the letter," Kat said.

"Once he realizes we're closing in, I'm sure he'll try it. We'll block him and try to get Charity to testify against him."

"Do you think she will?" Kat asked.

"That's what I'm turning over in my mind. She will have plenty to lose if she doesn't."

A House Divided

It was 9:30 a.m. when the front gate of Pastor Tom's compound swung open and his Rolls Royce Phantom emerged, turning right onto West Beach Road. A quarter mile away, a sheriff's deputy in blue jeans and a heavy parka watched through binoculars. He confirmed the only occupant was the driver, then bent his head toward his left shoulder and spoke into the microphone of his body radio. "All clear. One on board."

"Roger," was Shane's one-word reply.

Shane and Kat were sitting in their car a mile away at Fort Ebey State Park. They had been watching the big waves of wind-blown ocean surf crash ashore, and having a philosophical discussion about happiness.

Shane quoted his grandfather's advice, which he had found in a letter his grandfather wrote a century ago. "Make yourself useful. Then I think you should be happy."

"I've never been able to improve on that thought," Shane said. "We all want our lives to be fulfilling, and to make a difference. Whether it's by volunteering, or the career we choose, I think we're happiest when we are doing something for others."

She sat silently and thought for a moment. "So here's a question for you, does it make Pastor Tom happy to defraud thousands of people and then run away to a secret home in the Bahamas? Can you be happy if you just exploit people, and if no one respects you?"

"I doubt it," Shane said. "I think it's the only life he knows – he's a narcissist. Deep down inside, I think his life is empty and meaningless. Most people would think about protecting their good name, but he doesn't have one, and having one doesn't mean anything to him."

"We'd better go," Kat suggested. "We could talk about this all day."

"The board meeting should tie up the pastor for a couple of hours," Shane said. He started the engine and headed for Pastor Tom's compound. At the gate he rolled down his window, pushed the button and spoke into the microphone.

"Charity, this is Detective Lindstrom again. My associate Kat and I need to speak with you and it's urgent."

A few seconds later she replied, "Okay," and buzzed them in.

They pulled up behind the Jaguar, got out and rang the bell. Charity answered in pink yoga pants and bare feet.

"Yoga," she said. "Doing stretches. Come in and have a seat." Shane and Kat chose the sofa. Charity sat in a wing chair across from them, with her bare feet on an ottoman. Shane thought she had youthful feet.

"What is this about?" she asked.

"I'll get right to the point," Shane said. "We have a witness who has positively placed your husband and his car at Grace King's home at the time of her murder. We have additional evidence that he plans to leave shortly for the Bahamas, with Grace and you, to live in the home you have built there, and abandon the church he has built here. As it stands right now, you are an accessory to murder and probably also to embezzlement of church funds. Do you have anything to say about that?"

Shane saw put her hand to her head, cringe and mouth the word "no."

He continued, "So you are in very deep trouble, facing the prospect of spending many of your best years behind bars. No doubt your inclination is to stand by your husband, and I fully understand if that's what you choose to do. But I'm here to offer you another way that could save you a great deal of personal hardship. Work with us. Help us close the case against him and we will ask the court for leniency in your sentence. I have no doubt they'll look favorably on your cooperation."

Tears rolled down her face and smeared her mascara.

"I'm going to murder him."

Kat glanced around the room, found what she was looking for, and handed Charity a box of tissues.

"Thank you," she said.

Charity pulled several from the box, dabbed at her eyes and cheeks, and cleared her throat.

"First of all, I don't know what you're talking about," she blubbered. "Do we have a home in the Bahamas?"

"Yes."

"Is it nice?"

"Very nice, from what I can see in the aerial photography," Shane said.

"Well it's news to me. Tom hasn't said anything about moving there with me. If he was planning to go with Grace, that's something else."

Now, Kat's mouth hung open, too.

"Indeed he has a house on a private island, with its own airstrip. When we came into possession of the evidence, we did some checking with Bahamian authorities and confirmed all the details. It is the only home on Prosperity Island and is quite spectacular. We've also determined he has a very large account in a Bahamian bank. You didn't know about that?"

"No. Does Charlie know? The board president. Have you talked with him?"

"We're in the process of doing that."

"This means the church is finished. Did my husband clean out the account?"

"It looks that way – the church account and your personal account."

Charity shook her head. "That weasel! That absolute, sniveling, two-timing weasel! Yes, I'll work with you. I'll do whatever you ask to put him behind bars."

"There's one thing you could do for us right now if you don't mind," Shane said.

"Gladly."

"Could you give us something that would have your husband's fingerprints on it."

Charity looked up at the ceiling, and then got out of her chair and walked into the kitchen.

"I know what," she said, opening the dishwasher, retrieving a coffee mug and handing it to Shane. "Can you get prints off of ceramics?

"Yes, excellent ones," Shane said.

"This is his coffee cup from this morning. I haven't run the dishes yet. He likes to hold it with both hands to warm his fingers, so it should have a full set for you."

"Thank you," Shane said.

"He has Reynaud's Syndrome, you know – that causes cold extremities."

"I didn't know, but I'm sure the Bahamas are just the place to stave off the symptoms."

*

At Paine Field Regional Airport in Everett, Washington, a Grumman Gulfstream business jet taxied to the terminal area and spooled down. Pastor Tom watched the copilot lower the stairs. Then the pastor walked out to the aircraft, carrying a small suitcase and his laptop.

"Is that everything, sir?" the copilot asked, pointing to the suitcase.

"Yes, I'm traveling light today." He walked up the stairs. When he reached the cabin, he turned and went forward to the cockpit, where he reached for an envelope in the jacket of his sport coat and withdrew two five-hundred-dollar bills, one for each member of the crew. "Direct to Prosperity?" he asked.

"Direct," the captain said.

"We'll stow your bag in the cabin with you and be on our way in just a few minutes. The copilot did a brief inspection of tires, flaps and stabilizer, then ascended the stairs and pulled them up behind him. He walked forward to the cockpit, strapped himself in, and pulled a laminated checklist from the pocket on the side of his seat. He and the pilot spent the next few minutes going over the checklist aloud. Then they started the engines and taxied away from the terminal.

Moments later, the Gulfstream roared down the runway to the south and lifted into the sky. It made a wide arc to the right over open water and then over Possession Point and Freeland. Pastor Tom looked down at ferryboats, forest and beaches, and the homes of some of his congregation. The plane continued to turn until it was headed southeast.

Tom took his last look at Whidbey Island. He had given everyone the slip and it felt good. Tomorrow, Pastor Tom would be Tropical Tom, the Beachcomber.

Night Vision

George King balanced himself near the top of a twenty-foot aluminum extension ladder. It was propped against a fir tree more than a century old, judging by the last time this land had been logged. The height made him shaky but he did not want to admit this to Nadya, who stood at the foot of the ladder and steadied it. Trees have a way of putting human lives into perspective. This one had been growing here since the Civil War. If a man fell off a ladder propped against this tree and died, it wouldn't even be a blip in what this tree had seen.

Nadya understood now why George had been busy in his shop for the last two days. UPS had delivered a mysterious parcel to him earlier in the week.

"Are you sure this is safe?" Nadya yelled up to him.

"Of course. People climb ladders every day."

George reached into the tool belt at his waist and removed a cordless drill, and began to work. He had mounted the camera on a dark piece of board and needed to anchor it to the tree. He found a place for it that was nearly hidden from passers by on the ground, but that would allow the camera to sweep a field of view that covered the entire area where Zeke Kapinski had earlier watched his house.

"He will probably be back," George told Nadya, "but this time we'll be ready. This camera has night vision and will feed a continuous live picture to my computer, where it will all be recorded and entered into memory. The next time Kapinski gets any ideas about spying, we'll take the evidence to the sheriff and have him arrested."

For good measure, George had already installed a pair of

motion-detecting spotlights on a time delay that would turn night into day, startling Kapinski when he thought he was sneaking around in the shadows. But before the spotlights switched on, George's webcam would have gathered all the evidence he needed. The lights were just for shock value.

Betrayed

"This just gets crazier and crazier," Kat told Elizabeth over a glass of wine before dinner. "Pastor Tom apparently was preparing to skip town to the Bahamas with Grace, but had not told Charity a word about it. She is furious and chomping at the bit to testify against him."

"This has come so far from where it started," Elizabeth said.

Kat added, "You can't make this up. Don't you wonder how people get headed down such wrong roads in life – Pastor Tom, George King, Zeke Kapinski, Cordell Wurm? It's all so unnecessary and self-defeating."

"I think about it all the time," Shane said. "In most cases the wrong turn probably happens by little degrees, over years and years, the result of a thousand decisions in their life. For whatever reason they lack that internal regulator that most other people have, that keeps them on the right side of moral behavior, and society's expectations and norms. Once they cross over that line, we come along and try to understand why."

Kat sat and stared at the fire. She knew that understanding what shaped and motivated each of their suspects was the key to solving the murder. Grace King had either been a target of opportunity or represented such a great threat to the killer that he had to murder her.

George, her husband, had an undeniable motive to get Grace out of the way before his girlfriend arrived, but the more Kat learned about him, the more she saw complexities and contradictions that defied easy generalization. He had a way of shading the truth. Maybe that's actually true of most people – they skew the facts to present themselves in the best possible light. Only when pressed do they admit the whole truth. George seemed benign enough, and seemed to be searching for the same basic happiness that eludes so many in life. Notwithstanding all that, the evidence against him was overwhelming and damning. He'd have to explain it somehow.

Zeke Kapinski, the neighbor, was a self-confessed voyeur and had probably murdered his own wife two years ago. He had abundant opportunity to enter the house while George was away. And he was so short, if he were going to bludgeon Grace, it would almost have to be while she was lying down. Kat found him pathetic, but knew it would be a mistake to underestimate him. He had probably gotten away with murder once. Would he be foolish enough to try it a second time?

Cordell Wurm, Shane's go-to suspect, could well be the serial killer responsible for the other murders, and maybe even this one. He'd grown up in a dysfunctional home with no father and an alcoholic mother. With no one to guide him toward responsible adulthood, he'd made bad choices from the beginning. He had a hot temper and was quick to blame the other guy when something went wrong.

Then there was Pastor Tom, quite intriguing. He was a man of enormous talent and charm, an articulate speaker who could rally thousands of believers to his cause. Why had he chosen to go down the road of defrauding people for a living? Was it just narcissism and ego? Did a sense of superiority and invincibility drive him to exploit the gullibility of others? What could he possibly gain from risking everything on murder?

Elizabeth broke the quiet spell in the room.

"Where is the pastor now?"

"Home, I suppose," Kat said. "We're getting ready to haul him in for questioning."

*

"He hasn't come home," Charity said when she called Shane at 7:30 pm. "He left the board meeting when they broke for lunch, telling the directors he had a couple of short errands to run before heading home. I think he has already fled."

Shane's mind was racing. Prosperity Island had a six thousand foot runway. Knowing Pastor Tom, if he was on his way to the

Bahamas it would likely be on a leased private jet that could take him straight there. The nearest regional airports with business jet service were in Skagit County, Bellingham and Everett. Shane called each one, explaining he was tracking a fugitive wanted for murder and embezzlement, and asking security officers to look for a Rolls Royce in their public parking areas, and to check flight plans for any business jets that had left their field bound for the Bahamas today.

At Paine Field in Everett, he got lucky. Security already had noticed the unusual luxury car, a Rolls Royce, in short-term parking near the terminal, and a Grumman Gulfstream had left at 3:30 p.m. with just one passenger. The flight plan was for a destination at a private island in the Bahamas.

The jet would need to refuel en route, and it would be too late anyway to land in darkness on an airstrip with no lights. Shane figured they'd spend tonight on the ground somewhere en route, waiting for daylight.

Technically, the pastor should go through customs and immigration in Nassau, but Tom was used to special consideration. Shane guessed he had slipped this crew a little extra to fly him directly to Prosperity Island. The airstrip there did not have landing lights, so arrival would need to be after sunrise. Shane probably couldn't stop him now, but he had one more fallback.

*

The sun was just rising over the Atlantic Ocean as the Gulfstream passed over the southeast coast at thirty-five thousand feet and left the U.S. mainland behind. The sky was blue except for a few puffy, white clouds. Minutes later, Pastor Tom heard a change in the engines' whine and felt the jet bank gently to the left. He noticed changes in the flaps and knew the crew was starting their descent in preparation to land. The increased drag caused some vibration in a flight that had been quite smooth until now.

He was dreaming about spending tonight in his tropical paradise, listening to the palm fronds rustle in the warm breeze. It was a comforting sound he hadn't heard since leaving New Zealand. A local couple, his live-in caretaker and cook, would see to his meals and housekeeping. He had hoped to have Grace's companionship here, but instead there'd be some other pretty girl, flown in from one of the neighboring islands. A massage and some quality time with a woman would relax him after the last twenty-four hours of travel and tension.

He sensed he had gotten away from Whidbey Island just in time. The police were nosing around and would begin to put the picture together sooner than he expected. Their visit to his home had made clear the urgency of his situation.

He hadn't noticed the crew of the Gulfstream close the cockpit door. It had stood open for most of the flight. With essentially calm winds this morning for their approach, Tom was pretty sure they would swing out to the east, turn and come back to land to the west, so the pilots would not have to look into the blinding sun as they touched down.

The plane was descending quite rapidly now. He could see boats on the water below, then individual people on deck, and all of a sudden they crossed over a sandy beach and the view changed to palm trees and houses.

The houses were not right! There was no population on Prosperity Island, and this place was too big. They passed over neighborhoods and streets, people going about their everyday lives, as the jet dropped lower and lower, then screeched as its tires made contact with pavement. He felt the nose drop and then heard the roar of reverse thrust as the jet slowed and turned off the runway toward the terminal building.

"Welcome to Nassau," said a large sign over the terminal. The jet taxied toward it and stopped on the apron between Delta and Bahamasair. The engines shut down and the cockpit door opened as the copilot stepped into the cabin.

"What's going on?" Tom asked. "I thought we had an understanding about flying direct to Prosperity Island."

"All I can tell you, sir, is that we need to go through customs here. Bahamian authorities raised us on the radio and instructed us to divert to Nassau. We don't know much more than you, but there should be a local representative waiting here on the tarmac to explain it."

Tom had a bad feeling about this. They knew more than they were telling him.

The copilot lowered the stairs and three police officers in uniform came up the steps to the cabin.

"Sir," one of them began, "we have a request from United States authorities to detain you here on a charge of murder and a request for extradition."

Pastor Tom shook his head as they cuffed his hands behind his back and led him off the plane. "This is outrageous. Don't you know who I am? There has been some mistake."

What the pastor didn't know was that Shane had the thumbprint to prove that there wasn't.

*

Donovan waited on a leather-and-chrome love seat in Charlie DeGroot's real estate office and flipped pages in *Conde Nast Traveler* while the receptionist filed her nails. The scrape of the nail file was making his flesh crawl.

He heard a tone on the intercom on her desk and some incomprehensible muttering.

"Mr. DeGroot will see you now."

The two men shook hands and DeGroot signaled Donovan to be seated across from his desk. As he sat down, Donovan couldn't help noticing a large, framed portrait of DeGroot's parents on the wall behind him. Charlie looked to be about fifty years old, and had his mother's penetrating eyes and his father's bald head.

Donovan began by informing DeGroot that Pastor Tom had fled Whidbey Island and was under arrest in Nassau, Bahamas.

"That's impossible," DeGroot said, his expression suddenly of disbelief. "I was with him just yesterday at a church board meeting."

"As board president you probably ought to know what's happening." Donovan explained that the pastor owned a home on a private island, and was on his way there when he was arrested. "I need to confirm a few details about your own movements the last few days, since you are now in charge of Prosperity Bible Church."

Donovan asked where DeGroot had been on December 23 and 24, and who could provide an alibi for those hours. DeGroot said he was alone, going over the church books in the church office, and that no one had stopped by while he was there.

"I'm glad you brought that up," Donovan said, "because we believe there are some irregularities in church accounting and we'll be wanting to discuss those with you and perhaps others on the board.

Detective Shane Lindstrom has a warrant to enter the church and seize the books, so we expect your full cooperation."

DeGroot gave him a sour smile.

While Donovan was meeting with DeGroot, Shane and Kat hurried back to meet Charity at the sheriff's department. The white Jaguar was parked in the closest "Visitor" space to the front entrance, and Charity was already waiting in the office for them when they arrived.

"Your husband has been detained on an extradition request in Nassau," Shane told Charity. He wondered how she was feeling about the OBEY HIM license plate now.

"Thank the Lord," she said.

"Things happened so fast in the last twenty-four hours that we didn't get a chance to take your statement," Shane said.

Faithful to her promise to testify fully against her husband, Charity waived her right to an attorney. The church had been a sham, she said, based on a model they had used successfully before, in New Zealand.

No one would deny Tom was an articulate speaker who knew how to say just what his flock wanted to hear. He was especially good at reading people and giving them hope and inspiration. As his wife, her job was to play a supporting role they had carefully scripted for these performances.

Charity explained that when they married, Tom had promised her a lavish lifestyle and he had made good on that beyond her wildest dreams. She knew he had an insatiable ego and an eye for other women, but even Charity found him irresistible when he turned his charm toward her. Despite the womanizing, she thought he had a commitment to her that went beyond mere lust. Above all, they were partners.

To her humiliation, he pursued every beautiful woman who came through his the church, while piling up ever-greater financial gains from his scam. He had been siphoning money from cash donations into their personal account for years. She was totally unaware of the Bahamas house and his plans to abandon the Whidbey Island work and go there. She felt betrayed by that, because they had always been partners.

"What about Grace King?" Shane asked.

"It was pretty obvious Tom was interested in her, and also that things weren't going smoothly with her. He went to her house the evening of December 23rd to reason with her and didn't come home till the next afternoon. When he got back there was blood on his shirt and pants. He said their conversation had gone badly and he'd killed her in her sleep so she would not bring us down. He said she didn't suffer. He told me he'd done some things to deflect suspicion toward George King."

"Did he say what those things were?"

"That he'd found the keys to George's truck in the ignition and used it to transport her body, so the police would find blood in the back. He said he also left a blood stain in the garage, and that he battered her face to make it look like a crime of passion and rage."

She stopped talking to let Shane catch up as he scribbled notes on the conversation. He was also recording it.

"What's going to happen to me?" Charity asked.

"I can't tell you exactly," Shane replied. "But if you're being as honest as you appear to be, you'll come out of this in much better shape than if you had withheld testimony."

*

Kat dialed the number and waited. On the fourth ring, Robert Yuka picked up. "Haraldsen residence. Robert Yuka speaking."

"We got him!" she said.

"You got the murderer?"

"Yes, a charismatic, evangelical preacher – and a snake," she added. "And we disturbed some other snakes, too."

"Wow, I wouldn't have guessed it would be a preacher. Shane was pretty sure it was a suspect he'd been watching for the serial killings. You and Shane have been busy. Let me tell the others." Kat listened as Robert filled in Marie, Brad and Irene. She could hear whoops and cheers in the room.

"They think you did good work," Robert said. "But it pains me that we missed out on all that."

"Oh, I'll bet you had a wonderful time in Stanley, even without a case to solve. What have you been doing?"

"Well the highlight probably was a hayride to Redfish Lake on a sleigh, that Bolivar arranged. He even serenaded us on the harmonica." Bolivar was the Basque foreman of the Haraldsen Ranch."

"That is so cool."

"What's next for you and Shane?" Robert asked.

"I'm going back to school. I'm really fired up now to complete my criminal justice studies. I learned so much this Christmas. As for Shane, we uncovered a whole nest of suspects with shady secrets, so he may have some more arrests to make in the months to come."

Capitalist Bliss

George King awoke to a female voice singing something in Russian, acapella, in the kitchen. The voice was pretty but the lyrics were beyond him. Singing was one of Nadya's endearing qualities. George put on his robe and staggered down the hall. Nadya was brewing coffee and singing as she polished the stainless steel stovetop.

"What are you so happy about?" George asked.

"They caught the guy and it wasn't you."

"Did you ever doubt me?"

Nadya started to reply, but stopped short. She reached for the carafe and poured him a cup of black coffee. He sat down at the table and took a sip.

"This is good," he said. "Bold. What is it?"

"KGB Blend," she replied, laughing. "From Costco. At home we can't get."

"What were you singing?"

"Is Kalinka – Melinka, song from when I am little girl. Make me happy."

"Is nice. Geeze, now I talk like you. Do you always clean when you're happy?"

"Happy makes it easier. If I scrub floor, I am *really* happy. Come here, you big imperialist lug," she commanded, giving George a tight hug. She kissed him passionately on the mouth and cheeks, working her way around to an ear and the back of his neck, leaving big smears of red lipstick on his face.

"You have lipstick on face," she said. "Is ok."

"What's for dinner tonight?" George asked.

"Meat – from Costco."

"That reminds me. I have a surprise for you," George said. He crossed the room and opened the door to the garage. A Golden Retriever puppy came bounding into the kitchen and launched itself into Nadya's arms.

"I get dog," George said. "Now, we walk."

Nadya laughed as the wiggly dog smothered her in kisses.

"Can he sleep in bedroom?" she asked.

"Absolutely. We'll flip a coin to decide which of us takes him outside at 3 a.m."

Nadya gave him a sideways glance. "In Russia, dog is man's work."

"If I take him, we will bond and then he will only sleep on my side of the bed."

Shane had called George the previous evening to inform him he was no longer a suspect. The department had built a solid case against Pastor Tom, wiping the grin off his face, and he was in custody in the Bahamas, awaiting extradition.

The news lifted a great weight from George's shoulders, but he thought it lightened Nadya's heart even more. "I have not been a perfect man," he said, "but for you I am going to do better." Maybe, he thought, fairy tales can come true for lonely men and little girls with princess dreams.

*

Charlie DeGroot raced through the options. Should he lay out the whole sordid mess to his lawyer and hope he could wangle enough defense to get him the lightest possible sentence? Try to cut a deal with Shane Lindstrom to testify against Pastor Tom? Call an emergency meeting of the board? It might only raise questions he was not prepared to answer. He could hang a sign on the church, "No Services Today – Pastor Out of Town." How long would the congregation buy that?

He could try to line up a retired preacher to fill in, but could not begin to imagine who could fire up the congregation even a fraction as much as Pastor Tom. DeGroot could preside this Sunday himself, give some lame explanation for the pastor's absence, repeat some clichés and make a special, heartfelt appeal for donations. Since Pastor Tom apparently had looted the church's account, any additional income they could generate at this time would be crucial to digging them out of the hole.

But beyond everything, he was tempted to run, since his own complicity in the pastor's financial corruption was sure to come to light.

Tom had stabbed him in the back. DeGroot was sure Shane Lindstrom was riding high at the prospect of putting another member of the DeGroot family behind bars.

*

On the bridge of the *MV Kennewick*, Captain Gail Walker watched as her helmsman guided the ferry expertly into Keystone Harbor and the boat kissed the dock lightly.

"That was perfect," she said. "Absolutely perfect." She high-fived him.

She watched as the deck crew secured the boat and the shore agent raised the traffic arm. A handful of foot passengers trudged up the ramp to the waiting room, and then a deckhand waved for the first lane of cars to begin unloading. Every move they made was sharp, precise and efficient, just the way she liked it.

Walker watched as a big motor home and a Penn Cove Mussels truck rolled ashore, followed by a white sedan stenciled "Island County" and a logging truck that made this trip often, from Zeke's Wildcat Logging. The driver, a colorful character, had a white beard that cascaded down his chest. She thought he looked like a gnome and wondered what the story was on this guy.

Walker had long felt that one of the best and most important parts of her job was developing the skills of her crew. She kept them sharp, always mindful they might have to perform in an emergency someday. She expected a lot from them, but she was also a generous and supportive teacher.

Her thoughts often turned with sadness to her friend Grace, whose life had ended far too soon, for no good reason. There was some solace in knowing it was not domestic violence that had taken her life, but that changed nothing. Captain Walker would not soon get over the death of her friend. She missed the chats they had shared by telephone at all hours.

Still, January always made her happy and optimistic. The days were getting longer now. The holidays, and the toll they took on the emotions, were behind her. Perhaps this was the year she'd be free of her ex forever. Her detective friend, Shane, had offered his help if she needed it, and she knew that he meant it. If the creep made one false move, she would call Shane.

*

Zeke Kapinski turned right as he drove off the ferry, passed Crockett Lake and Keystone Spit, and continued out to the highway. His truck labored uphill under the weight of a full load of fir logs he would deliver to LaConner tomorrow. There, the logs would be dumped into Swinomish Channel, to be rafted and towed by a tug to the mill. The radio in the cab blared with the country-western voice of Johnny Paycheck. Kapinski sang along: *"Take this job and shove it, I ain't working here no more . . ."*

At the highway he turned right, toward Greenbank and home. He was feeling relieved that the murder of his neighbor's wife had been pinned on the pastor of Prosperity Bible Church. He was astounded that a county cop like Shane Lindstrom had taken down a guy who drove a Rolls Royce. The heat was off him now about this murder and also his wife's disappearance in Forks. He did not expect to see Lindstrom or his female sidekick again.

He could watch TV tonight and smoke Camels in his modular home, but could not help thinking the real show would be happening next door. George King and that buxom Russian girlfriend of his were just a short walk away, through the woods. It was after dark now and the lights of their house should illuminate what they were doing nicely. Maybe he'd take a walk over that way with his binoculars and just have a look.

No harm. No one would ever know.

*

Pock pock. Pock pock pock pock, Kat typed on her iPhone. She hit "send."

"Where are you now?" came the reply.

"Sitting on my bed at the Eagles Inn."

"Wish I was there with you.

"So you miss me?"

"Yes."
"Good. I'll be home soon."
"How soon?"
"A day or two."
"Absence makes the heart grow fonder.
"I've heard that."
"Did you have fun?"
"You wouldn't believe it. I'll tell you when I see you."
"XXXOOO"
"Same back atcha."

*

Nadya sat and stared at the email, in Russian.

George walked through the room and caught a glimpse of the incomprehensible Cyrillic text from the corner of his eye. "What in the world?"

"Answering email from my friend Vanya," Nadya replied. "She wants to know if I find Costco."

"Yes," Nadya had typed. "Shop there every month. Is nice place, America. Good prices."

Of course, what Vanya really wanted to know was what was happening in Nadya's love life.

"Is he Prince Charming?"

"Is long story," Nadya replied. "Prince need some work. I am bringing him around. Plan to get married."

"I am happy for you."

"We get dog. I name Valentina for first woman Cosmonaut. Take Tina to walk at Greenbank Farm."

Nadya looked up at George from her computer.

"We should invite Vanya to wedding."

"Ok with me," George said. "She could be your bridesmaid."

"Who would be your best man?"

"I don't know. Maybe Shane Lindstrom. I don't know if he'd even do it."

"He'll do it," she said. "I talk to him – use charm."

*

On Prosperity Island in the Bahamas, Kweku Standish swayed

in his hammock with the tropical breeze. His straw hat covered most of his face but he could peek through a slit under the brim, to watch the blue ocean. His wife, Adwoma, sat beside him in a lawn chair, enjoying her umbrella drink. They both wore polarized sun glasses.

"Ah, woman, dis is the life, eh?" Kweku spoke.

"That it is."

"When the sun gets lower, maybe I'll go fishing."

On the horizon, he watched a schooner under full sail cross his field of view. He and Adwoma could often see boats in the distance, though few came close to Prosperity. It was marked as private on most maps.

It was still two more weeks before they expected the mail boat, *MV Island Girl,* bringing their paychecks, groceries and supplies. Their paymaster, the rich American's lawyer in Nassau, had called them last night on the short wave radio to say that the island's owner had been en route to Prosperity, but was detained on an extradition request back to the United States.

The lawyer did not know when the American might be freed again to travel. But no worries, there was plenty of money in the management account and the lawyer would continue to pay them to keep everything in top shape.

So, the lawyer said, just relax and enjoy the good fortune of island life until further notice. Their pay and employment would continue without interruption.

*

Billy Lindstrom ran up the steps of the Eagle's Inn, into the arms of Kat Brown. "It's good to see you," she said. "I can't get over how much more you've grown since the last time."

Billy lowered his head and stared at his shoes for a moment, and then up at Kat.

"You look different," Billy said.

"I've grown out my hair."

"It's pretty."

Billy's mom, Judy, hung back with Shane and Elizabeth, and gave the two space for their reunion.

"So I've been dying to ask you, what's your favorite subject these days?"

"Ornithology," Billy said without hesitation. "But they don't teach that in school. I just read books."

Shane turned to Judy. "Thank you for bringing him over," Shane said. "Kat really wanted to see him again while she was here."

*

Cordell Wurm sat on a threadbare sofa in his mom's garage, in a haze of marijuana smoke. He smiled at the absurdity of his drug den. On one side of him sat the hot water tank, which was hissing. On the other side were the washer and dryer. This place was a dump. The dryer was running with a *thunk-ka-chunk* each time the drum turned over. His mom was probably passed out in the living room. Half a dozen empty cans of Pabst Blue Ribbon lay on the floor, and his eyes kept wanting to close. His mom's beer was horse piss but at least it was alcohol.

He hated that old cow and her fat cow daughter, whom he hadn't seen since she ratted on him in high school about the pregnancy.

He could party at his own house, but the police watched it so closely it was safer to do his relaxing here. Besides, he could bring his laundry.

A mouse ran across the floor and disappeared behind some boxes and tools in the corner. Did that really happen? He wasn't sure. He had smoked or snorted meth before each of the murders, and it often put him into an hallucinogenic frenzy. He wasn't sure what was real and what he had just imagined. He'd snorted a little tonight and experienced one mild high already. He planned to have a lot more shortly.

Wurm knew that the serial murders had tied Shane Lindstrom in knots. It was Wurm's way of getting even for a lifetime of police harassment and persecution going back to high school. The murders were a cat-and-mouse game, and he was good at it.

The pleasure was in carrying them out right under Shane's nose. He wondered how much Shane had agonized, trying to link him to the murder of Grace King over Christmas. He hoped Shane and his colleagues in Coupeville had wasted a lot of time and worry on it.

He already had some ideas about the next victim, which would be Shane's ex-wife, Judy, the mother of his son. That would shake

Shane to the core.

Judy was a float nurse at the hospital, and a party girl, and Wurm was pretty sure he could pick her up if he put himself in the right place and used his charm. She was a cocktail-hour regular at several restaurants on the island that had good bars.

He had been watching her for days, forming a picture of her routine. Wurm knew all about the conventional wisdom that many serial killers want to get caught, but he really didn't want that; he just wanted Lindstrom to know what he had done, and that there wasn't anything he could do about it.

Wurm picked up a large packet of methamphetamine from the battered coffee table in font of him. He turned the packet over and over in his hands. He had bought the drug from a new supplier, who promised him it was extra pure and powerful.

Finally, he poured the crystals out on the table. They were beautiful. He could grind and snort them, which he often did, but today he really wanted to smoke them. He had the sniffles from too much snorting, anyway.

Meth gave him a rush of euphoria, but he had built up a tolerance. Over time it was getting harder and harder to get that rush, and he had increased the dose to compensate. One benefit of the drug was that he could go long stretches without eating or sleeping. He had lost weight and he supposed it had something to do with not eating.

But his teeth hurt like hell, which further decreased his desire to chew and eat. He had lesions on his face, which he had picked at, making his skin unable to heal. His cheeks had become sunken. A psychiatrist he had seen while in jail warned him meth was not only damaging his mouth and teeth, but his nose and lungs as well, and fueling his anger, irritability and aggressiveness. If he continued to use it, he would die an early death.

He could care less.

He could always numb himself with something to make the pain go away.

In fact he was already in a pleasant daze from the marijuana and beer. Wurm studied the white crystals that held so much pleasure. He picked up a small glass pipe from the table and packed it full of crystals, and started to smoke. He could feel his heart speed up as the chemical reached his bloodstream.

Moments later he was asleep.

At seven forty eight p.m., Cordell Wurm awoke momentarily and convulsed several times. His chest heaved, and then his heart stopped and he moved no more.

The clothes dryer continued to run – *thunk ka chunk, thunk ka chunk.*

Champagne

Shane, Kat and Elizabeth sat around the big oak table in the dining room of the Eagles Inn B&B, their faces aglow with candlelight. A cozy fire crackled in the woodstove.

Kat looked around. "I'm going to miss this place," she said.

"It's going to feel awfully empty after you go," Elizabeth replied.

Elizabeth picked up a bottle of champagne, pointed it away from the group, and released the cork with a pop. She filled three glasses.

"To Kat and Shane," she said, raising her glass. "You caught your man." They clinked glasses all around.

"I don't know," Shane said. "We caught a murderer, but not the one I was after. We learned that the guy next door to the victim's home, Kapinski, is a voyeur and probably also a murderer who has gotten away with it up till now. And we uncovered massive embezzlement in the largest church on Whidbey Island, which will take months or years to sort out. Thousands of people are suddenly without a church, and no doubt their faith has been badly shaken. The whole thing comes full circle back to the DeGroot family, who never seem to be far from corruption."

"It's not a neat and tidy business," Kat said.

"No, but there's one thing you can usually count on."

"What's that?" Kat asked.

"Humans are creatures of habit – remarkably predictable. Whatever we've done before, no matter how self-destructive, we will probably keep right on doing it until something forces us to stop. Habits and addictions are terribly powerful. Human nature is something we just can't change."

"I'd like to stay and help you catch that serial killer," Kat smiled, "and pin something on DeGroot, but I really must get back to school. Do keep me posted on both of those."

"I forgot to ask, do you have a love life these days?" Shane asked.

"Shane!" Elizabeth exclaimed.

"We got so busy I never thought to ask." He was lying about not thinking about it because, for days now, he'd been watching Kat smile as she answered texts. He just hadn't found quite the right moment.

"Dear god!" Elizabeth blurted. "Aren't you being a little nosy?"

"Kat and I don't have secrets. We can talk about anything, like two adults," Shane said.

"Well . . ." Kat said, "there is someone I miss very much and want to get back to see. Now that I've fought off Pastor Tom and seen what lovebirds George and Nadya have become, I'm thinking a little more romance might be nice."

"Is this guy you've been texting good enough for you?" Shane asked.

Elizabeth looked up again. "Listen to you! Aren't you being a little over . . . protective?"

"I just want what's best for Kat."

"She's an adult. Isn't that what you just said?" Elizabeth asked. "She's a pretty good judge of people, I'd say."

Kat sat there and watched the two carry on.

"I suppose you're right," Shane conceded.

"And if she needs any help sizing up men, she should talk to me, not you," Elizabeth added.

"Well since you won't be happy until you know his name, it is Guy," Kat said.

"That's his name? What kind of name is Guy?"

"He reminds me a lot of you, Shane – strong and caring, with impeccable integrity."

"Oh. Well then he's a pretty solid guy."

"I'll keep you both posted on any announcements about my love life. In the meanwhile, Shane, give yourself credit."

"For what?"

"You cleared George. He and Nadya are happy as two clams. I think they'll live happily ever after. When this started I wouldn't have given them much chance. Charity is free of her two-timing, sleaze ball husband. That's something, though I couldn't guess what she'll do with her life now. Speaking of the sleaze ball, he's behind bars and due back here soon to answer for his crimes. So that's not a bad holiday's work."

"That's right," Shane said. "We did all that over Christmas break."

"I noticed," Elizabeth remarked.

"Let's have a toast to Kat and Guy," Elizabeth said, raising her glass. Shane and Kat clinked it.

Just then, Shane's cell phone rang. "I'd better see who this is," he said.

Obituaries

"I don't know why we even subscribe anymore," Elizabeth said as she flipped pages in the thin south island newspaper. "There's nothing in it, especially in these holiday editions with all the canned 'Year in Review' pages."

Then she added, "Well at least the obituaries are fresh. My god, get a load of this:"

Dr. Joyce Harcourt – Coupeville audiologist, Dr. Joyce Harcourt, 34, died in a one-car accident Christmas Eve at Deception Pass Bridge. She was pronounced dead from internal injuries at the scene. The Harcourt Clinic is now closed until further notice.

Grace M. King – Greenbank software developer, Grace King, 35, died Christmas Eve as the result of a homicidal attack in her home. She is survived by her husband George King, and a sister in Montana. Services are pending.

Cordell Wurm, 26, of Clinton, beloved son of Mrs. Patricia Wurm of Freeland, went to be with our Lord, January 1. Death was from accidental causes at the home of his mother. Cordell attended South Whidbey High School, where he participated in football in his freshman year, and the South Whidbey Catholic Church, where he served as altar boy. In 2010 he was foosball champion at Joe's Tavern. He is survived by a son, Jesus Wurm, of Dutch Harbor, Alaska, and leaves behind many friends. Cordell had been working on the island as a roofer's assistant. At his request, his remains will be cremated and there will be no services.

"Can't you find something more uplifting to read?" Shane asked.

"Sure. How about the social notes? 'Miss Vanya Ivanova of Chelyabinsk, Russia, is visiting Greenbank this week for the wedding of her best friend, Nadya Komanesch, to widower Mr. George King. Miss Ivanova will serve as Miss Komanesch's bridesmaid, and Detective Shane Lindstrom of Freeland will be Mr. King's best man. After a brief service, a private reception will be catered by Costco of Lynnwood."

"It doesn't really say that, does it?" Shane gasped.

"I might have ad libbed a little."

The Brad Haraldsen Mystery Series

Available from Whidbey Island bookstores and online from Amazon.com in
paperback and Kindle versions.

| Book 1 | Book 2 | Book 3 | Book 4 | Book 5 |

Final Deception: *A Whidbey Island Mystery*

In the blackness, Bella Morelli pitched face forward in an
ungainly dive, wind roaring in her ears. The four seconds took
forever and she had two last thoughts – surprise and dread. She hit
the water all wrong like a breaching whale, lungs first, a horrible
impact, and that was the last she felt.

*

Deception Pass Bridge connects Washington's Fidalgo and
Whidbey islands across a deep chasm. It is 180 feet from the bridge
deck to the water, depending on tide. From there it's 130 more in icy
darkness to the bottom.

A young person in peak condition, hitting the water feet first in perfect form, can survive if they miss the rocks and regain the surface before drowning or hypothermia. A 67-year-old cannot. Whirlpools and eddies reach out to clutch and pull them down.

*

Decades ago Brad had almost cracked the mystery of Bella. She had taken a road trip with him, taken a risk. Brad registered them in a Tennessee motel as Mr. and Mrs. Brad Haraldsen.

They hadn't discussed the sleeping arrangement – it just happened. They were two unmarried 25-year-olds traveling in the South in 1972. Gatlinburg was a honeymoon destination and the couple's eyes glistened with new love. Even in civilian attire, Brad carried himself with military bearing. That and his clean-cut, neatly trimmed hair were assets in the South where patriotism ran high.

As it was, the clerk didn't question their marital status – gave them a room by the pool in the nearly vacant auto court.

A heavy sky threatened afternoon lightning. Brad and Bella swam anyway and washed the miles from the road. Then, five years into their friendship, they made love for the first time as comfortably as if it were every day.

The lovemaking was slow and satisfying, their private secret as the storm rumbled through the lush hills beyond the thick curtains. Afterwards, they lay in each other's arms. Bella smiled and Brad felt her caution about him wash away.

A lifetime later, sitting on his mountain in Stanley, Idaho, Brad still teared up at the memory, as vivid now as it had ever been. That time, that place to which they had never returned, was the happiest of his life. Brad's eyes stung and he closed them to see it all again. He remembered every detail of that motel, that room, the long journey that led there.

Final Passage: *Mystery on the Alaska Ferry*

The Matanuska inches ahead between flashing navigation buoys in Wrangell Narrows, changing course at each marker to stay within this twisting channel. Evening is falling and a campfire burns brightly on shore a hundred yards away. Sweet smoke from the fire drifts over the ship and takes Brad back to times he and Irene spent in the mountains of Idaho with their friends of a lifetime, Stu and Amy, both now gone. It's a bittersweet memory.

Brad imagines a family around that campfire, roasting weenies and marshmallows, or maybe good friends talking about their day. Smoke drifts toward the ferry from woodstoves in cozy cabins so close they could shout to the owners. A dog barks. A couple standing on their deck wave to the ship and Brad waves back.

Petersburg is a storybook scene on this quiet night. Irene is glad she made the effort to stay up. The lights of the town and its many boats must hold a thousand secrets of ordinary people and their Alaska-size dreams on the edge of the civilized world.

Moonlight bathes the snowfields of nearby peaks. This is the prettiest place she has seen on this trip, a pocket of humanity in the heart of wilderness, surrounded by water, mountains, glaciers and forest. She has this moment to herself, the other passengers having retired to their cabins for the evening. She lingers a while, then starts a leisurely circuit around the deck, taking in the view and the aromas of creosoted pilings, fish canneries, fir trees . . .

The impact from behind knocks the wind from Irene's lungs and sends her reeling forward, fighting for balance. She grabs wildly for the rail with her right arm and barely catches it, staying half on her feet, unable to breathe. Her heart pounds and her legs fold. She wraps her body over the rail and gasps in shock, staring down at the white bubbles where the bow slices through the blackness. Half a minute passes with no air. She's in full panic.

Then, ever so slowly, her diaphragm responds and her lungs draw air. She straightens up and wonders what happened. She is alone on the deck – no passengers, no crew. The ship already is in open water, accelerating toward Juneau.

Final Escape: *Mystery in the Idaho Sawtooths*

On the porch after dinner, Brad breaks out two Mt. Borah Brown Ales for Shane and himself while Elizabeth and Irene clink glasses of wine. Brad notices Elizabeth looks especially beautiful in the soft light of the early evening, her long red hair catching the sun. Did she fix herself up a little extra? He catches Shane's eyes lingering on her.

In the distance, the soulful melody of a harmonica floats their way on the breeze.

"That's Bolivar," Brad says, "introducing Billy to the harmonica. He's not bad, don't you think?"

Brad explains to Shane that the ale comes from a small craft brewery in Salmon, several hours north. "I think it's a delicious beer and it brings back memories of the time I climbed Mt. Borah in the Air Force."

"You were 20-something?" Shane asks.

"Yeah. About that."

"Reliving past glories," Shane laughs.

"Exactly."

Irene interjects. "He has a rich fantasy life."

Brad stares at her with a knowing smile. "I happen to like my fantasies," and then back at Shane. "Seriously, Shane, while Billy is with Bolivar and we have a few minutes, I wanted to ask your advice about a problem Elizabeth is having."

Shane leans forward and listens while Brad outlines the situation. When he finishes, Shane leans back and turns to Elizabeth, "Is it the same guy?"

"I don't think so."

"Because of the black hair? The pony tail?"

"Mainly that."

"I think it might be him," he says. "Otherwise it's an awfully big coincidence. It wouldn't be a hard disguise."

Brad adds, "There's something else. I didn't mention this to Elizabeth earlier, but we've started getting some harassing phone messages and hang-ups here at the ranch."

"What are the messages?"

"To keep our noses out of other people's business."

Final Justice: *Mystery on Whidbey Island*

At the clearing's edge, where the tall grass and brush gives way to trees, a man begins to dig. It's a remote spot some distance from an isolated building at the end of a private, forest lane nobody uses. Sweat runs down the man's forehead from his bald head and stings his eyes. From his back pocket he extracts a red bandanna and ties it across his forehead.

The man digs three large sword ferns with generous root balls and sets them aside on a tarp with the rest of the dirt from the hole.

A feeling grows inside him that he's not alone. Heart pounding, he stops, straightens up and looks around for something that does not belong. He scans the trees and shadows, and suddenly registers two large, yellow eyes and sharp-pointed ears staring right at him.

It's a Great-horned Owl thirty feet away in a fir tree, backlit in the shadows. The owl follows every move; its eyes unnerve him seeming to know too much.

The two being study each other, neither breaking his gaze. Then finally, the man turns his back and returns to his work. With a pick he breaks loose a little of the coble and scoops it out of the hole with his shovel, then goes back to the pick. He feels those eyes watching the back of his head.

Final Pursuit: *Mystery in the Adirondacks*

Something brushed Shane Lindstrom's shoulder as he slept.
His wife, Elizabeth, lay beside him and he was pretty sure she'd
touched him on purpose – lightly, so as not to startle him. The bed
was deliciously warm and he willed himself not to move. He didn't
want to awaken. When she did it a second time, it was sharp.

"Somebody's in the house!" she whispered urgently.

"Huh? He mumbled, turning to face her.

"Didn't you hear it? A window sliding open downstairs."

"Are you sure? Not just the breeze?"

"There's no breeze."

Shane glanced at the café curtains in the bedroom window,
dimly backlit by a quarter moon. They hung straight and still on this
humid night. Beyond them lay Pursuit Lake and a handful of cabins
linked by shoreline trails. How could anyone be prowling downstairs?

. . . The next sound was unmistakable – a metallic crash and
muffled moan in the kitchen below them. The moan was human and
Shane was wide awake now, too. He pictured someone lowering
himself through the pantry window from the screened deck, probing
for the floor with his dangling feet and kicking the galvanized pail
Shane had left by the window in preparation to mop the floor . . .

Shane folded back the sheet, swung his legs out of bed and
stood. . .

Stepping into his pants in the darkness, he fastened his belt,
then slid open the bedside drawer and felt for the reassuring bulk of
his Glock. In the drawer beside it was a high-intensity tactical
flashlight, which he slipped into his pocket. It could temporarily blind
an intruder.

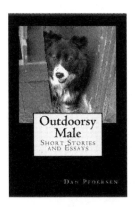

Outdoorsy Male: *Short Stories and Essays*
Available from Amazon.com and Whidbey Island bookstores

Don't Photograph My Wattles

"I have only one vice," my old kindergarten classmate announces as she fishes a pack of American Spirit cigarettes from her bag and lights one.

A blue cloud engulfs us as we huddle under an awning in a chilly October-morning rain. Tammi has just finished a sesame bagel with cream cheese at the Bakery by the Sea in the quaint village of Langley, Whidbey Island.

"Well that sure was disappointing," she declares, screwing up her face.

"The bagel?"

"Yeah. Not that good."

"I sneak a glance at my watch because we are already late to the workshop she is presenting this morning."

"You say this is the only bakery in this backwater?" She asks.

"Only one."

"Crap."

Nodding at the cigarette pack in her yellow fingers, the points out, "At least they're all natural." She smiles for the first time this morning. "No artificial additives. No genetically modified tobacco."

Then she adds, "You can stop looking at your watch because I'm not going to rush this."

The smoke, which clings to us like burning tires, saturates my blue jacket and gray beard.

We are getting reacquainted after Tammi's first night in my garage guest apartment. I haven't seen her for about 60 years. She asks for a wakeup call, which I place to her iPhone at the stroke of 7:45.

"Yeah, I'm up," she answers with a voice like gravel, then apparently goes down again.

It turns out Tammi doesn't like the fruit and one-minute oatmeal I've stocked for her in the Guest Apartment by the Sea, nor the coffee. "I'm not an oatmeal fan, she says. "And to be honest I just didn't feel like cooking breakfast this morning." So at the last second she asks if I will drive her someplace for a bagel.

"I don't do dairy, sugar or wheat," she declares. "Or GMO."

As an afterthought she adds, "You only get one body."

I am struggling with every part of this.

Standing in the weather, she fills in a piece of her story. "My life is the shits. I know the reason I'm not wearing a ring on this finger is because I'm a nag. Well, that and some other things. That alcoholic turd I married wasted my best years. I've got nothing to show for it now but a bad back, a mountain of debt and a pack of dogs. I have this fantasy I'm going to meet a nice man on Whidbey Island, marry him and live happily ever after."

She sucks another lungful of smoke and blows it all over me.

"God, I hate being poor," she says. "I have no backup. Why does everyone else lead a charmed life but me?"

"It's all luck and timing," I say.

"I hate my gut," she remarks. "I swear I'm going to lose this spare tire. I know you plan to take pictures at the workshop. Keep in mind, I don't photograph well. I wave my arms and that makes my wattles hop around. Do not photograph my wattles."

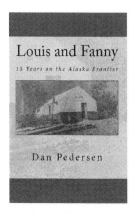

Louis and Fanny: *15 Years on the Alaska Frontier*
Available from Amazon.com and Whidbey Island bookstores

Trees sagged under a blanket of white. Boots kicked up powder in the streets of Seward, Alaska, as the mail steamer *Dora* pulled away from the dock. The ship trailed a plume of black smoke. Captain C.B. McMullen stood at the stern, taking a last look at civilization and pondering what he'd find on his return to Kodiak.

He'd just reached Seward with a firsthand account of conditions in the remote outpost of Kodiak. Mt. Katmai had exploded 100 miles from Kodiak in a volcanic eruption that was still spewing ash into the atmosphere. The *Dora* had called on Kodiak after tense hours sailing blind in conditions that could have cost McMullen the ship and all aboard.

Now he was going back with the minister's wife.

*

On Kodiak Island, ash filled the sky and blacked out the town for 60 hours. Landslides of ash swept away houses. People went hungry and expected to die. Lightning struck the Naval radio station, setting a fire and knocking out communication with the outside world. Ships' radios were useless with the electrical disturbance.

Townspeople waited in darkness, their eyes and throats burning with dust, wondering if they could survive this, whatever it was.

Downwind, ash rained for a day at Juneau, across the Gulf of Alaska. In Vancouver, B.C., more than 1,000 miles from the volcano, people wondered if the sulfuric atmosphere was safe to breathe. It all happened just as the *Dora* was completing its westward run, bound for Kodiak a few hours ahead. It waited offshore till conditions cleared enough to approach Kodiak . . .

*

"The day was an exceptionally beautiful one and we were all on deck enjoying our cigar and the scenery when someone shouted: 'Look at the smoke.' Gazing off to the westward we beheld across Shelikof Straits, on the mainland, an immense column of smoke ascending skyward, its diameter seeming to be at least half a mile or a mile."

The volcano was 55 miles from their position, and Thwaites went on, "Of course we all thought of our cameras, but the distance was so great that the idea of securing a photograph was abandoned as impractical. We continued to watch the phenomenon when it began to dawn upon our minds that it was rapidly becoming dimmer, and that a dark mass of cloud was showing above the column, mingling with it and coming our way."

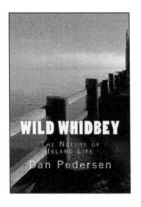

Wild Whidbey: *The Nature of Island Life*

In Full Color
Available from Whidbey Island bookstores and online from Amazon.com

People argue in circles about whether islands attract a certain kind of person or create them. I think it's both, but skewed toward the latter 30 years into my one-man study.

We make our big turns in life for complicated reasons, including luck and self-delusion. I had some romantic ideas about island life and they played a role in my irrational move to Whidbey Island when I still had a fulltime job in the city. I saw something wholesome here, wasn't sure how to explain it or get it, but hoped I'd figure it out . . .

The move was impulsive but soon became transformative . . . Waking up in a blissfully quiet place, I wasn't prepared for the birdsong. The woods act as a megaphone an hour before sunrise, when all the birds awaken with something to say. The songs change with the seasons and I started correlating the changes with seeing the first Rufous Hummingbirds of March, the first Violet-green Swallows, the first Black-headed Grosbeaks and Western Tanagers, even Great-horned Owls on foggy winter nights.

The spring migration is nature's timeless cycle. It's a barometer of how we are doing on this planet and takes place alongside but separate from our human concerns. To me it is comforting and reassuring amid the constant chaos of our world – war, crime and breaking news, politics, terrorism, jobs, divorce, drones, sickness, smart bombs and talk radio, and all the other noise that spews stress at us.

As time passed I started caring more about the cycles of nature than the cycles of news. In this I am well aware I am not normal or typical of most people and how they live . . .

I started counting the growth rings on the century-old tree rounds I was splitting, imagining the seasons those trees had seen. I found friends who cared about such details as much as I did. And I discovered the luxury of silence – the simple joys of a book and a camera, and some time outside.

Whidbey Island's abundant wildlife and forests, gentle people and creative community all claimed parts of my soul. All shaped my values and philosophy, and my temperament. I grew accustomed to kind smiles and cheery "good mornings" from both friends and strangers on the sidewalks of Langley and the trails in our woods. I stopped worrying about the person coming toward me in the dark.

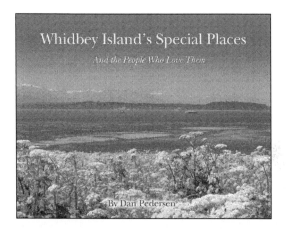

Whidbey Island's Special Places
And the People Who Live There
Available from Whidbey Island bookstores

Standing in the shadows of giant old-growth firs and cedars at South Whidbey State Park, Elliott Menashe remembers a story. It's about a woman who attended one of his classes on forest management.

"She was imperious – a real tough cookie," he says, shaking his head. He'd been telling the class about forest snags and all the reasons to leave them intact as wildlife habitat, but the woman was not buying it. "I've got a 60-foot snag that's about six feet thick. "It's annoying me and I want it gone."

Menashe asked if it was a safety hazard. "No." And was it full of woodpecker holes?

"Yeah, it's got those. But I want it gone."

"You just moved here, right?" he asked, then offered her a deal. "Leave it alone, and in a year if you don't change your mind, I will pay for its removal."

About a year later a package showed up in Menashe's mail.

"It's a bottle of really good wine. Chocolates. And pictures of, you know, baby owls, eagles, osprey, herons, kingfishers – all these pictures. She said, 'If you hadn't stopped me I would never have known what I was doing. Thank you so much. I look around me now with different eyes.'"

The story illustrates an error Menashe sees often as principal of Greenbelt Consulting, a natural resources consulting firm. Newcomers often don't seek advice about living in harmony with nature. Arriving on the island from an urban or suburban setting of traditional lawns and landscaping, and with little previous contact with wildlife and woodland processes, their first impulse is to clear a big view, eradicate native vegetation and replace it with neat, manicured suburbia.

In the process they destroy all the best, most wondrous and magical reasons to live on the island.

A good place to become immersed in those wonders is the mile-long Wilbert Trail, across Smuggler's Cove Road from the entrance to South Whidbey State Park. Parallel parking for several cars is available at the trailhead on a widened section of road shoulder about 0.4-mile north of the park entrance. It is marked with a crosswalk and a small sign identifying the Wilbert Trail.

"This is not a true old-growth forest," Menashe clarifies. "It's a mature forest with old-growth remnants." The distinction is important but takes nothing away from the impact. A few steps from the highway, hikers enter a sea of sword ferns. Several hundred feet later they come to a mammoth Western Red Cedar, next to a bench on which to sit and contemplate.

"The Ancient Cedar" is estimated at 500 years old, but Menashe says it's probably not the oldest tree on this trail. Altogether, only about 1 to 5 percent of old growth forest remains in the Puget Sound Basin, and Menashe says every bit of it is priceless and deserves to be saved.

. . .

FINAL IMPULSE

ABOUT THE AUTHOR

Dan Pedersen grew up in Western Washington. He holds two journalism degrees from the University of Washington and worked as a reporter and editor for several newspapers in Idaho and Washington, including a large outdoor weekly. He also managed publications for a financial services corporation. He is the author of ten books, six of which are mysteries.

He writes a weekly blog about nature and rural living, Dan's Blog, at www.pedersenwrites.blogspot.com.